What happened at the House.

When I moved to the city, I took the first available room in the city...one that was available, thanks to a nasty breakup. The room was fine, the rent reasonable, and my roommate and I got along while allowing me to save up for an apartment of my own. I thought I'd hit the jackpot, until, before I had enough, his ex came crawling back and pushed me out.

To assuage his guilt, my roommate gave me a lead for a room in an older home, one where all the renters were "just like you." I assumed they meant bi, but after falling in love with the place and giving my deposit, I discovered what they really meant—this was a house full of littles and me? I wasn't even sure what that meant, not really.

I have two choices, confess or cross my fingers that no one figures it out. I choose the latter. It's not like I would ever betray their trust or try to ruin their good time. I knew what it was like to be the one not accepted and I wouldn't wish that on anyone. And besides, the longer I'm here, the more I wonder if maybe I am little after all.

Their Little House Boston is the third book in the Five Little Roommates series by USA Today bestselling author Della Cain and her bestie Kaytea Kat. Boston is an M/M/M daddy little romance featuring not one but two littles, the daddy who loves them both, a house full of littles with no daddy in sight, a bisexual first time little, bottles, stuffies, onesies, true love, an adorable dog, the day at Chained that changes everything, chickie nuggies, mischief, and all the fun and sweetness you have come to expect from Della and Kaytea. If you love your daddies sweet, your littles fun, and your HEAs wrapped like a hug, grab Their Little House Boston today.

The unauthorized reproduction or distribution of a copyrighted work is illegal. Criminal copyright infringement, including infringement without monetary gain, is investigated by the FBI and is punishable by fines and federal imprisonment.

Please purchase only authorized electronic editions and do not participate in, or encourage, the electronic piracy of copyrighted materials. Your support of the author's rights is appreciated.

This book is a work of fiction. Names, characters, places, and incidents are the products of the author's imagination or used fictitiously. Any resemblance to actual events, locales or persons, living or dead, is entirely coincidental.

Their Little House Boston
Copyright 2025 Della Cain and Kaytea Kat
Digital ISBN: 979-8-89320-200-7
Print ISBN: 979-8-89320-201-4

Published by Decadent Publishing LLC

Also by Della Cain

Collared by Love series
A Puppy for His Little
A Master for His Puppy
A Family for His Daddy

Collared Ever After series
Litigation and Lace
Lollipops and Leashes
Lipstick and Lecture Halls
Contours and Cuddles
Manties and Muffins
Sculptures and Snuggles
Pacis and Photographs

City Daddy, Country Little series
Purple Rein
His Little Sunshine
Touch of Gray
Blue Jean Night

His Crimson Skye
Precious Zane

Faking It series
Happy Faking Plus One
Merry Faking Christmas

Other Titles
Daddy's Little Christmas
Daddy's Little Christmas List
His Boss's Little Christmas
Daddy's Little Christmas: Aster
A Daddy for Christmas: Hermie
A Little Christmas: Claus's Secret

By Della Cain and Kaytea Kat

Found by Daddy Series
Bridger's Lost Duckie
Jeremiah's Lost Paci
Archer's Lost Onesie
Austin's Lost Fireman

Easton's Lost Otter
Owen's Lost Hero
Gordon's Lost Mitten
Walker's Lost Lollipop
Lane's Lost Kitten
Colby's Lost Binky
London's Lost Engine
Reid's Lost Cap
BJ's Lost Crayons

Five Little Roommates

Their Little House Colter
Their Little House Tristan
Their Little House Boston

Also by Kaytea Kat at Decadent Publishing

A Little Christmas: Timmy
A Little Christmas: Dash's Secret

Their Little House Boston

By
USA Today Bestselling Author Della Cain
And
Kaytea Kat

Chapter One

Boston

The headlamps of the bus were heading my way, and I ran as fast as I could, barely getting to the stop on time. It was the last bus of the night for this route and, had I missed it, I'd have been screwed. The cost of a taxi the distance I was going would be astronomical, if I could even find someone willing to travel that far this time of the night.

I'd been stuck at work, finishing a project that wasn't even mine. My coworker gave their two week notice and was told that they were no longer needed, effective immediately. If they weren't needed, I wouldn't have been working past midnight to get their shit done. No one would call me the perfect employee, but when the boss begged for someone to take it over, I was the first one with my hand up after they changed the offer from comp time to overtime.

I didn't need another day off. I needed cash. I was saving up to get an apartment of my own, or maybe a small house. Something that didn't require a forty-five-minute bus ride to work or sharing a space with someone who was fine but not a person I'd choose to spend time with.

I plopped into my seat and braced myself for the long journey home. The smell of the bus was every bit as ripe as you'd expect at this time of night—stale beer from some drunks who'd been wise enough not to drive, the faint smell of puke, and, of course, a whole lot of body odor. But the bus was a cheap way home, and it wasn't like I'd been expecting elegance.

The ride felt extra long and I nearly missed my stop, thanks to my bright idea to close my eyes, "just for a minute." If the driver hadn't slammed on his breaks, I'd have been forced off at the last stop on this route with no bus back.

"Night." I gave the bus driver a nod on my way off and popped into the twenty-four-hour convenience store across the street from the place I'd been calling home to get some very overdue dinner. All of the hot food was either long gone, or, in the case of the pizza slices, far past their time to be tossed out. I ended up grabbing a questionable turkey sandwich out of the cooler and a bottle of lemonade before jogging across the street and up the four flights of stairs to my apartment.

I'd only been there for a month, and the place wasn't horrible. I'd have loved an elevator, especially when moving in, but the landlord kept the hallways clean and lit, and the neighbors were quiet. There were far worse places I could be.

My roommate Ray wasn't a friend, or even an acquaintance until we moved in. That had been a first for me. I preferred to either live alone or with someone I knew and liked. But I was no longer in my college town and knew exactly zero people here when I took my job.

It was a jump scare seeing the rent prices here. If it was only the rent I had to think about, I'd probably have sucked it up and snagged a place of my own and taken on some side hustles to make ends meet. Moving in cost so much more than that. Most places I inquired about wanted first, last, and a deposit. I was looking at big bucks from the get-go, and one thing I didn't have was big bucks.

Ray's ad in the local marketplace had seemed too good to be true. He had a private room that didn't require first or last month's rent. He didn't even ask for a deposit or lease. The listing raised every red flag there could possibly be. That was probably why it was still available. When I finally sucked it up and inquired, my one-month relocation benefit at the extended-stay hotel about to expire.

I didn't have high hopes, or any hopes really. I figured best-case scenario was in a not-so-great part of town. Worst case? It had rats and roaches, and I'd need to walk through an area I should never be in after dark, and there was mold. Thankfully it was none of those things. Ryan was nice enough, the room wasn't too bad, and the price was great with no hidden anything.

He'd been through a really bad breakup, and his girlfriend moved out. From the sound of it, I'd have done the same exact thing she had. He'd slept with his boss, of all people. But that wasn't for me to judge, especially not when I was the one fully taking advantage of the situation like a little vulture.

I'd been very up front with him from the time we met, letting him know I liked both men and women. I posed it as a question pertaining to overnight guests, a litmus test I'd read was solid in an article about roommate hunting while queer. In theory, it was known to keep me out of what could quickly become a pretty ugly situation.

If he said I could only bring home women, they were biphobic, and I didn't need that in my life.

Thankfully Ray didn't pull that. He said as long as we kept it in my room, he didn't care who I brought home or how many, but that the living room was off-limits to all guests without prior approval. It wasn't ideal, but at least he didn't send me packing, which was better than moving in and finding out later they were assholes.

I went straight into my room. Normally I wouldn't eat in there, but I knew that if I made too much noise in the kitchen by opening cabinets or even shutting the garbage can a little too loudly, I'd disturb my roommate. And the last thing I wanted to do was piss him off. Not signing a lease went both ways. It allowed me to move out without notice, but it also allowed him to kick my ass to the curb in the same manor.

Living here had been great as a stopgap. I was about halfway to my savings goal for an apartment. But if I could stay here longer without the commute killing me, I might even have enough for a down payment on a small house.

I ate my sandwich quickly and climbed into bed beside my stuffed koala. I barely had the light off when I realized my roommate wasn't alone. Their bed was creaking, and the moan was definitely female. I grabbed my earplugs, popped them in, put on some lofi, and went to sleep thinking maybe he'd moved on from his ex.

It wasn't until the morning, when I walked into the kitchen and put my pot of coffee on, that I saw who it was. He had not come close to moving on. This wasn't some random one-night stand or a girl he just started dating. Nope. It was his ex. I recognized her from the picture he showed me when he sobbed about what a dumbass he was.

"I'm Boston." I somehow made the moment more awkward with those two words. *Ugg*.

"My boyfriend said you were staying here for a little while."

Boyfriend. That was not the word I wanted to hear. Boyfriend meant they were back together. Boyfriend meant my bedroom, the one that had once been her office, might no longer be mine.

"Yeah." What else was there to say?

"Thanks for helping out with the bills while I threw my fit of temper because he made a mistake."

Mistake. She called him putting his dick in his boss a mistake. This situation was going from bad to worse. He'd somehow managed to gaslight her into thinking this was her fault.

From the sounds of it, my days here were limited…very limited.

I pressed the button on the coffee maker. "Excuse me, I need to catch a shower before work. Nice to meet you."

The next day, my roommate told me she was moving back in in two weeks and would need her office for work. And that was fair enough, but also, that didn't give me a lot of time.

"I'll start looking," was the best I could offer. I not only needed to find a place without the cash most complexes needed, but had to find one with immediate availability.

"I know this sucks, but I got you," he said and handed me a little pull-tab flyer with a phone number on it. "It's a room for rent in an older house. You'd be one of multiple renters, but they're all like you. I'm sure you'll get along."

"Like me?"

"Yeah, like you with your preferences."

Oh. He meant they were queer. That was one hurdle skipped. And at least he was trying?

"Well, thanks. I'll give them a call."

I didn't really have a choice, and besides, it had to be better than being homeless. Right?

Chapter Two

Elliot

"Hey, Elliot, before you leave for work, I need to talk to you."

My stomach dropped. I hated when *people needed to talk* to me. Mostly, I loved people. They were quirky and weird, every single one of them. Especially the ones who were trying so hard to be what they thought was normal.

But, from my parents, I'd learned that necessary conversations were usually about something I'd done wrong.

I hoped that wasn't the case with Monroe. I liked living here at this sanctuary he'd made for us littles.

"Of course." I took a few calming breaths.

"It's okay." Monroe clapped me on my shoulder. "I didn't get your rent this month. You're always so punctual, I wanted to check in on you."

I cocked my head to the side, confused. "I paid the rent, Monroe."

His thick eyebrows bunched above his nose. He was attractive, but I saw him as only a good friend. "Oh."

Then I remembered. I hadn't given him cash like I usually did. "Remember you said paying through the app is better for you? That way you don't have to go to the bank."

His dark eyes flicked to mine. A smile slowly formed. "I forgot I asked you to start that this month. I thought I was losing my marbles."

"Go on and check before I leave, just in case there was an issue. I sent the test deposit a few weeks ago, and you said you received it, but let's make sure."

Monroe pulled out his phone and clicked on the app. "There it is. Right on the first."

"I gotta run."

He smiled. "Go. Have a great day."

I waved to him on my way out.

As I pulled into the parking lot of our local library, my heart lifted. A lot of people in this world drudged to work every day. Dragging their feet. Grumbling all the way.

I wasn't one of those people. Sure, I reshelved books and watched over the study rooms. Every once in a while, there would be someone grumpy or someone who thought getting louder was the answer, but I loved being around books. They didn't disappoint you or treat you badly. They were there for comfort and information and to stimulate the mind and soul.

Being a librarian was the absolute best.

Since it was the heat of summer, there were more patrons than usual. More people typing on their laptops in air-conditioned private rooms. More kids coming in and out with parents. More books to shelve. I would sometimes open the door to the children's room to listen to story time from my desk.

I loved every second of it.

My shift ended at nine. We used to be open until ten but, with cuts in funding, we had to close earlier. The resulting dip in pay made me spend a little less on extras.

I took pride in being a good steward of my earnings.

At home, a few of my roommates were still awake, watching a movie in the living room.

Showered and changed into shorts, I made my way to the kitchen. The last thing I wanted to do was heat up the house even more than it was. We kept the air conditioner on a reasonable temperature right between being able to afford the bill and roasting.

I decided on leftover spaghetti, since it could be heated up in the microwave. I really wanted some mini corn dogs as well, but we were out.

Those were my favorite.

As I ate, my good friend Scottie came into the kitchen to fill his sippy cup with juice. "Do you want to play later?" he asked.

I glanced at the clock on the wall. "It's getting late, so maybe tomorrow? It's my day off."

Scottie nodded. We'd had several late-night talks about life and love. He was a good listener as well. "That sounds good, but I work in the morning. We have movie night tomorrow as well. All of us."

"Are you making your crazy movie popcorn for all of us?"

Scottie threw in gummy worms and Oreo crumbles. Everything he could get his hands on. He called it popcorn salad, but there wasn't a fresh thing in sight.

"Of course. It wouldn't be a movie night without it. See you then."

I had a mini ice cream cone before going to bed. While I brushed my teeth, I leaned against the counter and tried not to let the nighttime loneliness in. It already began to creep into my thoughts.

What I wanted to do was crawl into bed with a daddy who would wrap me up in his arms. Stroke my hair. Pull the blanket up over my ears like I liked it.

Someone to take care of me.

That was what I really wanted.

I hopped into bed and opened up my latest romantasy obsession. I could only read a few chapters at a time before getting tired at night, so this one book lasted over a month. Most people thought that librarians sat and read books all day long and got paid. Sure, I got to read sometimes but mostly, there was work to be done.

I sighed happily. Tomorrow was my day off and I intended to play my little heart out.

My days off were recharges for me.

My eyes began to close and I put my book on the side table and shut off the lamp. Going to bed would be a lot better with someone to cuddle with.

A whole lot better.

Chapter Three

Tripp

I hadn't slept past seven since Juno came into my life. She had big brown eyes, floppy ears, and the coldest nose I'd ever had thrust into my armpit first thing in the morning. When I adopted her at the local shelter event, they'd told me a lot about her. She had been about four months old, loved long walks, and would break into zoomies every time I let her out in the yard. Poor pup had been surrendered along with her siblings, and she was the last one of the litter still there.

What they didn't tell me was that I'd brought a morning person—morning dog—into my life. And that was not the life I'd been accustomed to leading. I got up early only for work, sleeping until noon on the weekends more often than not.

Still, I'd challenge anyone to say no to the cutest pup in the world. Even after three years, I couldn't think of her as anything but a puppy. She still had the goofy, sweet attitude. Together, we'd hiked all the local trails and some farther away, seen waterfalls I had no idea existed, even taken a weekend trip to the beach because I thought Juno might like sand and surf. Spoiler alert: at first, she didn't want any part of beach life, but, once I got out the Frisbee, she forgave me for getting her toes all sandy.

With a business like mine, it was hard to make plans far in advance, which meant I missed out on most group activities, and Juno was the perfect companion, ready to go whenever I was and never upset because I got stuck at the office and tickets to a traveling Broadway show went to waste.

It was also why I was single. I peopled all day at work, and sometimes that didn't leave enough of me for another person.

"Hello, girl. You know the sun is barely up?"

She bounced on the bed next to me, her brown, black, and white fur glossy in the early morning light.

"Do you need to go out?" Odds were that yes, she would like to go out and do what dogs do in the morning, but the main reason for the excitement was less biological function and more an interest in having fun.

I often thought that she had the right idea, but I couldn't come up with a way I could make hiking and Frisbee throwing into a way to pay the mortgage.

At least, with my own insurance agency, Juno could come to work with me most of the time, curling up under the desk by my feet and patiently waiting for her lunchtime walk and snack. Life could be a whole lot worse.

Before Juno, I generally ate at my desk or not at all, but, with her, I had a reason to leave the building and stroll down the street to the park on the next block. The deli on the block took phone orders and didn't mind if my furry cutie came in to grab my food, health department rules be damned. That half hour, sitting on a bench and eating a sandwich while Juno frolicked in the dog park with her besties: priceless.

After lunch, back to the office for meetings and paperwork before either waiting around for an evening appointment or going home to work out in my home gym, have something easy for dinner, and calling it a night.

Or, on rare occasions, Juno had a night on her own while I visited my club, Chained. As a daddy with no little, the little room there was an ideal location to find like-minded caregivers for a short chat or a little who wanted a daddy for a play session, no strings attached.

Chapter Four
Boston

When Ray told me the room for rent was in a large house, I formed a vision of something far smaller than what I walked up to. In its day, the building had probably been a boarding house or some city official home back in the day. The place was absolutely gorgeous and huge.

My initial concern had been that the rooms would be too small to accommodate multiple roommates. Taking in the architecture, I doubted it. The entire neighborhood was dotted with homes from a similar time period but none quite as large as this one.

I took out my phone and snapped a few pictures, thinking that maybe I might research the history. I'd always been fascinated by older buildings and, even if this hadn't been a potential new place for me, it would've caught my eye. Something about the place intrigued me.

I walked up and knocked on the door, skipping the bell, which felt far too modern for the carved masterpiece that was the entrance. As I waited, my imagination took off, and I envisioned the door being opened by a butler dressed in an old suit from years gone by. All the stories a building like this could tell.

But instead of the regal employee ready to announce my arrival to the owner of the home, a man about my age opened the door wearing jeans and a random T-shirt from a local restaurant. Far more relatable but not quite as fun.

"You must be Boston."

I nodded. "I am. Are you the person I'm meeting?"

"Yeah, I'm Monroe. I own this place—well, the bank owns...you know what I mean."

As he led me inside, he told me about how he inherited the home but had to borrow a lot of money to fix it up. Having roommates was a way to keep the building while not going bankrupt.

"And it's fun to have people to play with." He clicked the door behind us and gave me a minute to soak in the atmosphere.

It instantly felt like a home when I walked inside. Maybe not my home but one nonetheless. There was no apartment-complex vibe, so similar to a hotel. People lived here. It wasn't just a place to sleep.

He toured me through the grand living room and the kitchen that might as well be an entire restaurant compared to what I'd been used to. And then we went upstairs. "This is where you'll be if you decide to stick around."

The room was almost as large as my current apartment, if I included the en suite. I could easily set up a workstation, along with my bedroom set and possibly even a couch. Hardly mammoth, but compared to the places I'd been living since I graduated, close enough.

"All the rooms are different in configuration, but to keep things simple, we all pay the same rent. Even me."

That was interesting. Why would he pay rent to himself? To keep it fair, I supposed. It was nice to know he wasn't a slumlord—so many of them were sketchy as could be.

"We can go over the rules when we go downstairs. As far as visitors in your room, obviously, we want to keep this safe for everyone, so no one should feel uncomfortable in their own home."

I agreed with that. I might not be a huge fan of mega-rules, but also—when you lived together, you made compromises.

"Now, I'm sure you're waiting to see the playroom, so let's go."

He hadn't come across as a big nerd type, where there would be lots of video games or movies to the point they needed their own room, but I was fine checking it out.

I was shocked when he opened the door.

When he said "playroom," he didn't mean videogames or Lego. He meant basically something that looked like a nursery from a community center or a church. There were areas of toys, short chairs with tables. It was very much not what I expected.

I nearly asked if there were a lot of single parents who lived here. Thankfully, he cut me off before I put my foot in my mouth.

"You're allowed to play here whenever you want. If you want to dress little or dress in your normal clothes while you play, it doesn't matter. But there is a schedule in the kitchen if you want to have a daddy or a mommy come play with you. We really try to limit those times, again so people feel comfortable."

It took me a second to process—this wasn't a playroom for children. This was a playroom for people who were into kink. Specifically age-play kink.

I didn't know a lot about it, but it seemed pretty harmless as far as preferences went. I never yucked on anyone's yum, but I'd be lying if I said I was comfortable with blood or air play around me. Age play? Definitely not a deal-breaker.

"Do a lot of people use this area?"

"Of course. And if someone's in here, feel free to join. Part of the reason we only rent to littles is so that everyone feels comfortable."

Wait—they only rented to littles? Was that who Ray thought I was when he said there were "people like me"? Did he think I was little?

I wasn't. And I wasn't sure why he thought that. It didn't offend me or anything, but it was a bit confusing.

The right thing to do would be to leave. Tell him I was sorry I made a mistake and go.

But I had two days to vacate my apartment, and I was a safe person. I'd never be cruel or unkind about anything that happened here, and I for sure wouldn't tell anybody.

Maybe sticking around until I could get my own place wasn't the worst idea. There was no rule that said I had to be playing in this room. At least, not that I'd gotten indication of yet. I could come home, stay in my room, mind my business, and then, when it was time to move on, move on.

Their Little House Boston

It was far from ideal, but I already loved this house, and I could see myself being friends with Monroe.

Although...are you really friends if you lie about who you are?

Crap. This was a harder decision than I thought it would be.

"Let's go downstairs and review the rules."

"Sounds good."

Maybe the rules would hold the answers I needed and let me know if I could do this...or if it was time to find one of those long-stay motels. The kind where you had to jimmy a chair under the door handle in the hopes of keeping safe at night. I hoped it was option A. I really liked this place.

Chapter Five
Elliot

What a fun and relaxing day. I'd played video games in my room most of the time. I loved the cozy games. Stardew Valley was my favorite. Farming games were the best.

Tonight was movie night, and I wanted to get something real into my stomach before my obligatory handful or three of Scottie's popcorn salad, so I shut my console down and headed for the kitchen.

When I got there, someone was standing in the middle of the room, looking lost. He had short, wheat-colored hair and beautiful eyes. His hands were on his hips. He wore gray lounge pants and a navy-blue hoodie.

Attractive didn't even begin to cover how gorgeous he was.

"You must be Boston?" I asked.

He snapped out of his daze. "I am. You are?"

I barely quelled my giggle. "Elliot. It's nice to meet you. Monroe said we had a new roommate. I've been in my room all day."

He nodded. "Just moved in today."

The nervousness came off this man in waves. His gaze darted around the room, and bare toes tapped on the linoleum flooring. Being the new guy was never easy, and I wanted to help him feel at ease, welcome. "Have you seen the playroom? I have some time if you want to play before the movie starts."

Boston nailed me with a stare. "I don't know." Poor guy. Maybe he was new to the little life or he'd never been able to play before.

"That's okay. We don't have to. I was about to make some mini chili dogs on Hawaiian buns. Are you hungry? Wanna share?"

"I am hungry," Boston answered. "But I hate to take your food."

I waved him off. "Eating with friends is more fun anyway. Besides, we all share around here. It's not just a house, it's a community."

"That's nice. Can I help?"

We made mini chili dogs together, and I cut up some cucumber spears because vegetables add fiber. When we took the hot dogs out of the oven, Boston was practically drooling.

I had a strong urge to care for him for some reason. He was beautiful and nice. But he was a little like me. Others had throupled up before, but I didn't know if that was my fate. Besides, there wasn't a daddy to share. Or, at least, I didn't have one.

Maybe Boston did, but I needed to stop overthinking and making up futures with someone I'd just met.

While we ate, he answered some basic questions. Where he worked. Things he liked to do. I avoided the little subject because he seemed wary of saying anything about it.

I picked up our empty plates and started toward the sink. "Do you want to watch the movie with the others?"

His gaze went to the living room where the others were gathering for the show. Scottie would be in to make popcorn salad any minute. Littles didn't just sit on the couch and watch a movie. They brought out blankets, pillows, sleeping bags, and stuffies for the comfy community event. Most of them dressed in jammies as well.

"I don't know."

His unease made me anxious. I knew how it felt to be that nervous.

"Maybe I should go and unpack instead. It all seems overwhelming."

Their Little House Boston

Poor Boston. We could be a lot. I didn't want to assume things about him, but his trepidation made me think more than ever that he was new to this life. He would be okay around here. We didn't judge, and everyone lived at their own pace. It was the one place I knew of where we could be ourselves. Of course there was Chained, but as far as a place to call home, this was it.

"Can I see your room?" I asked. I didn't want to push him, but the urge to get to know him better guided my thoughts.

"Oh, sure."

We walked up the stairs together to his room. Boxes and totes lined one wall.

"How about I help you make your bed? That way, you at least have a comfy place to sleep tonight."

"That would be nice. Thank you."

He pulled out a neatly folded comforter and sheets, along with standard pillows. Some of us had cartoon or character bed sheets and comforters, but his sheets were plain baby blue and the comforter a basic white with thin navy pinstripes. We made the bed together, laughing over the messed-up corners of the fitted sheet. We got it wrong three times. This was why I insisted on stripes on my sheets. The stripes never did me wrong.

"Well, good night, Boston."

"Good night, Elliot. Thanks for…thanks for tonight."

"You're welcome. See you around."

I really, really hoped I saw him around.

Not wanting to spend the rest of the evening in the house, I skipped the movie and got dressed to go Chained. They had the best little room and had gotten a lot of new toys.

But, tonight, I didn't go to play, just to hang out. I met my friend Sammy there, and we had a drink. I was tempted to go to the little room, but I hadn't dressed for it, and I had a hard time getting into the right headspace without the clothes. The conversation area with its comfy couches and chairs was relaxing enough.

A few drinks in, I was ready to get home. I had split days off and a shift in the morning.

This little liked his sleep.

I took off and went back to the house but, before retiring in my bedroom, I stopped at Boston's door. The light was off. I sent a wish up to the gods that he

Their Little House Boston

was sleeping well and being here would somehow heal all of his nervousness.

I also wished we would be good friends.

Chapter Six

Tripp

Sometimes, even if I was tired, Chained was the only place to go to clear my mind. Over the years, I'd been a member, so many of the other daddies had become good friends of mine. I'd witnessed their meeting their littles at the club or once or twice at a munch, and seeing their relationships blossom had been a heartwarming experience. Every one of them deserved their happiness, and it was small of me to feel even a pinch of jealousy, but it was hard not to. I didn't want to take their joy, just hoped one day I'd meet the little who filled my empty cup.

The club was busy tonight, and I tagged along with Bridger and his little Hudson and a few other couples into the little room. Ms. Lily had an event going on, as she so often did, a themed evening. This time, it was called: Literature for Littles, focused on the many books in the library there, most of them picture books but a few a little more advanced for the middles.

Of course, there would be storytelling, but the books were just the base for the evening. The door to the little room was wrapped to look like a book titled *The Best Night Ever*. The window in the middle of the door was left unwrapped so a little or their mommy or daddy could see from outside what that night would be like.

Following Hudson across the room, we passed groups of excited littles and their caregivers gathered around the various activities, their laughter and chatter contributing to the atmosphere promised by the door wrap. As always, arts and crafts, building games, circle games, and others were available, but the clever Ms. Lily kept it from seeming ordinary. Our first stop was a puzzle station, where Hudson and his friends assembled a giant floor puzzle. It came together to reveal six special book covers.

"Where did she find this, do you think?" Bridger asked. "These are some of Hudson's favorites from the library here."

"Guessing special order," I replied, not even trying not to laugh as the second they finished, the littles took it all apart and mixed it up again. A few stayed to do it again, but Hudson and most of the others split up and darted off in different directions. "Looks like he found the glitter."

"Oh no." Bridger paled. "I am still getting the last of it out of his hair from the Teddy Bear's Picnic with Sparkles.

I chuckled. "The bane of daddies. The best thing about being single and just playing for an evening is that I don't have to deal with the aftermath of glitter." If that was so great, why did it make me nostalgic for when I did have a little in my life? Sure, it had been an effort to make sure the dignified banker would arrive at his office the next morning without the light catching any sparkles on his nose or ears, but it was also rewarding. He loved his bubble baths.

"I know what I'll be doing in the wee small hours." But he made no move to stop his little, who was gleefully gluing multicolored glitter onto a piece of poster board in an attempt to recreate his favorite bunny from a story, or at least that was what the club staffer in charge of the project had explained was the idea.

But his bunny... "Is it me, or does that bunny look more like a duck?" I mused.

Hudson wore a onesie patterned with yellow rubber duckies, bright yellow socks, and sneakers that had ducks that lit up whenever he stomped his feet.

Which he did often. He was adorable, and rapidly becoming sparkly.

Bridger leaned in and shook his head. "That's a duckie. But I guess it's not a big deal. He's having a good time."

Since the little was beaming and chatting with his neighbor while adding a beak to the "bunny," there was no question he was enjoying himself. "Creativity is important."

"Yes, it is."

Hudson finished his project and handed it to the staffer who clipped it to a cord strung across the wall, to dry. Then he was on his feet, stomping them a few times to light up his shoes. "Daddy, I want to play a game."

"Okay, my best boy. Which one?"

"That one." He pointed across the room to where littles sat in a circle while one ran around the outside, tapping shoulders. Maybe some version of Duck, Duck, Goose, probably changed to meet the theme. "Come with me, Daddy. You, too, Daddy Tripp."

"Thank you, Hudson, for inviting me. I think I'm going to go have a drink, though." I hadn't seen a single little who caught my eye, and it wasn't that much fun without a little to play with, even if Hudson and Bridger were allowing me to keep them company.

"Bye, Daddy Tripp." Hudson was already in the circle by the time I'd said my goodbyes to his daddy and started for the door. Other friends were equally involved in the fun, but I was done for tonight.

Outside the little room was a very different atmosphere, much more adult. Other rooms had their own activities. Like the pet room and some private dungeons and things, but when I emerged onto the main floor, it was to the area most of the members spent their time at Chained. As always, I was reminded of how much I liked the gentler air of the little room. It might be loud, and there could be paint on the tables and frosting on cheeks. Sometimes people left for diaper changes.

But out here where impact play held sway, along with fire, electric, and all the other kinds of activities most people associated with kink. The music was different, intense, and the lighting set to spotlight the submissive bound to the spiderweb. Those who knew better were not surprised by puppy play or littles whose evening was spent gluing glitter to poster board.

As I nursed my drink, a man a few stools down the bar caught my attention. He wore ordinary clothes, but something about him said little. Attractive, lithe, a sweet smile when he accepted his glass from the bartender. I was just about to go over and say hello when another man joined him.

Time to go home and tell Juno about my evening. Even she'd be bored by it, though.

Chapter Seven
Boston

It was great having Elliot help me unpack and get settled in. That time together made this feel more like a place I belonged than a room I was renting. For a few minutes, I thought I might go downstairs and join the others for movie night when I was done. Movies were fun, right?

But I chickened out, unsure what I'd see there. Were they going to be wearing diapers, sucking on pacis? Was it going to be a show written for young children or a horror movie or a rom-com? Would they have snacks I'd want to share or baby food? I didn't know what I expected from a social evening here or age play in general.

It wasn't the playroom, but that didn't mean I'd be prepared for what I'd see there. Everyone here, to their knowledge, enjoyed being little. Why would that be exclusive to one room? Or maybe it 100 percent was.

Instead, after Elliot said his goodbyes, I stayed in my room, wandering down to the kitchen when my stomach finally protested too much about being empty. I stopped by the movie night long enough to say hello and not appear like I was avoiding them. It was very different than what I thought it would be.

There were blankies and stuffies, many of which were not much different from my koala. They weren't necessarily baby or toddler toys like I half assumed. In fact, one of them had a huge bear sitting on an empty chair—I guess so he could watch too? I didn't even know who the bear belonged to, but he made me smile.

But as I scanned the room, Elliot wasn't there. Was that the real reason I'd made sure to put in an appearance? Elliot definitely was a factor, and not in the best way. I was attracted to him. Very. Mixing home and play was the epitome of bad decision-making, and I wouldn't act on it. But making good choices and shutting down feelings weren't the same thing.

Maybe he went up for the night, or he was in his room. As much as I wanted to see if it was the latter, I refrained. Being too needy wasn't going to open the door to friendship, and I wanted at least that from him.

Instead, I wandered in to the kitchen, made a cup of instant noodles to curb the hunger, and then went to bed.

A week passed, and I'd managed to avoid the playroom without coming across as weird or rude. I'd met all my roommates, even if just in passing, and every one of them seemed nice. But I connected most to Elliot. And not just because he was hot, although he was exactly my type.

Looking back on our few interactions, he intrigued me. He was little. He had to be if he was living there. The odds of two of us accidentally finding this place and keeping quiet were slim to none. Besides, he talked about little things in passing. Although, in a lot of ways, I'd have thought he had daddy vibes: he helped me with my room, cooked and cut things up for me, checked in to make sure I was doing well.

One day, I'd need to ask him about that. Maybe after I moved out and could share the truth—that I wasn't really little. If that was true. The longer I stayed here, the more I questioned if maybe I was. Not in the way these people were. I didn't ever act on it. But I'd be lying if I said I didn't appreciate the little things that Elliot did for me, things normal friends wouldn't.

My day at work had been long and boring, waiting for different test runs of our reports to go through before checking to make sure they were working properly. It was a lot of sitting, and with sitting came my brain wandering...straight to the playroom.

What harm could it do for me to go in there and try it out? Maybe I'd like it. It might be exactly what I needed. Or it could be awkward and weird, and I'd never have to do it again.

There were no rules to this, except for the one I already broke—the one where I signed up to rent a room in a house I probably shouldn't be living in. I was glad I did it, though. In so many ways, this place was perfect and I was already learning new parts of myself.

When I got home, I took a quick shower, wanting to wash the city bus off me. I grabbed the most youthful shirt I had, bought at an amusement park the previous summer, and a pair of pajama pants. It was hardly what anybody would call little attire, but it would work.

I'd already checked, and the little room wasn't checked out for any visitors for the rest of this month. It was safe. Still, I was nervous as I reached the door. I didn't want to share my first time there with all my roommates. The pressure would be too high. I wanted to explore on my own.

The lights were off when I arrived, which was good. I'd have at least some time to myself. I flicked them on and went around the room, taking in a book station, crafts, cars, and blocks—including the huge plastic bricks. That's where I started.

I stacked them aimlessly, no final project in mind. They were all squares and rectangles. There wasn't much I could build other than a wall, and before I realized it, all the bricks were used, and I had a very large wall of plastic in front of me.

That silly task, that playing, allowed me to escape from my own mind for that time. Was that how it was for everybody? Is that why they enjoyed this so much?

"I liked your tower."

My head snapped up to see Elliot in the doorway wearing footie pajamas and a huge smile.

"I thought I saw the lights on. Can I join you?"

I nodded, unsure what to say or how to say it. Was I supposed to be using a small voice since I'd already been playing? Was there a protocol to all of this?

We took my wall/tower apart and built it together again. After dismantling it, we didn't really talk, just adding one block after another, taking turns and enjoying each other's silent company. Once all the blocks were used, we took it apart again and stuck everything back in the bin. Block time was over.

Their Little House Boston

I was about to excuse myself to go to bed. This already had been a big deal for me, and I didn't want to push it. This time in here gave me a whole lot to think about.

But just as I moved to stand, Elliot asked me, "Can I read you a book?"

Like I could turn down that face.

I nodded, and we went over to the beanbags, sat down, and he grabbed a book about a koala, probably because he'd seen mine. Elliot seemed the kind of guy to pay attention. And I was right.

"Your stuffie's not here."

"I didn't know if we could bring our own toys, or if this was shared toys only," I explained. It was an actual thought that had gone through my head on multiple occasions during the short time I'd been here, so not exactly a lie. The logistics of the room fascinated me.

"It's always up to you. And you never have to share your special stuffies. Not ever." There had to be a story there.

Koalakins lived on my bed, and I did almost snag him but stopped short, unsure if I'd brave coming in here at all. Next time, I'd bring him with me. Because one thing I'd learned today was that there would be a next time.

He opened the book to the first page and read the words on it. He flipped to the next, but this time, he made up a story based on the pictures, not reading a single one of the words. I loved it.

It made the story exciting and new, even if it was completely ridiculous and not at all close to what the author intended.

Sitting there, listening to him read, being in this space, not having any cares in the world, at least for this moment, was comforting in a way I never expected, almost like a hug. It was also painful, my sides hurting from laughing so hard, especially as he read the third book. The voices he made… How could I help but join him.

But also, between the laughing and the listening, I was struggling. Struggling not to lean forward and kiss my roommate. Talk about the fastest way to complicate things.

I needed to keep my growing attraction to him under control before I messed up what was looking to be something great.

Chapter Eight

Elliot

By the time we got to the end, there were tears rolling down my face. Boston was so much fun. He ended up joining me in the character voices and even made sounds when they did things.

He was really a blast.

I put the book away but didn't want to say *the end* on our evening together. Not even close.

"I don't know if you're feeling up to it, but would you like to join me at Chained? Just a drink or two. I'm not in the mood to play but I could use a scotch."

Boston looked conflicted. His gaze darted around the playroom and he wrung out his hands. I thought for a second he was going to say no. Until he didn't. "You know what? I could use that drink. Sure. Let's go. I'll just have the one."

I shrugged. "My treat tonight. No worries. We have to get you approved as a guest, though. Let's get online and see if we can do it quickly."

"Approved?"

Their Little House Boston

"They really value their members' privacy. Last time I took a guest, it was very fast, so cross your fingers."

It was as fast as I hoped. I didn't know how they checked the info or what they were even looking for, but they were sure efficient. I shut my laptop lid. "So that's that. Meet me at the front door in ten?"

I noticed he took a moment to make sure the books were stacked in order of size and put his chair back under the table.

As soon as I was out of sight, I rushed to my room and picked out some nice jeans and a black button-down shirt. I didn't button it all the way, and then I rolled up the sleeves to the elbow.

With my phone and my wallet in hand, I made my way to the front door where Boston was waiting. Tapping his toe. Waiting.

He was a little like me, or so I thought. I shouldn't be taking him for drinks, but I couldn't help myself. Something inside me wanted to take care of him and love him.

I guess love didn't follow any rules.

"Ready?" I asked.

Boston nodded. "Yeah." We walked outside and got into my car. Boston cleared his throat and looked at me while I started up the engine.

"What?" I asked.

"Nothing. Not nothing. You look really good tonight."

"So do you."

We got to the club, and I headed straight to the bar with Boston following close behind me. When I stopped at a table, he bumped into me. "Sorry."

"It's fine. What's your poison?"

We spent the night at a tall round table, talking about my work, his work. Observing people at the club. We made up stories about people who passed us. Boston was really good at it.

Before long, our one drink turned into two for me and over five for my companion. He wanted to know more about me and my life as a little. How I knew the lifestyle was for me. If I had a daddy and if they were nice to me.

"I don't. I want one. I'm sure you do too. I just haven't found the right person."

"How do you know you've found the right daddy?" he asked.

I shrugged one shoulder. "I guess I'll just know. I'll feel safe and taken care of. Free to be me. Totally in love."

"What if something happens and you don't think you're a little anymore or maybe you never were."

I had a feeling we were no longer talking about me. Boston had more drinks than me and clearly was more than tipsy. "I'm sure my partner would love me for more than just my chosen lifestyle. I would hope they would accept me no matter what."

He huffed out a laugh.

"Did you want to go? I think you've hit your limit."

"I think I have too. My head is getting fuzzy." When one person told another they'd hit their alcohol limit, the answer told you a lot about that person. Alcohol enhanced anger. Deepened depression. Brought out the best and worst in people.

Boston leaned on me as we walked out of the club. I got him into the car and turned on the heated seats in case he got cold. He went on and on about how cute I was and how he liked spending time with me.

I told him the same things, but I was sure my words fell on deaf ears. Or drunk ears.

Either way, the next day, he wouldn't remember what I said, but I would recall everything.

Back at the house, I helped him to his room and then into his pajamas. He giggled a bit as I tucked him into bed.

"What are you laughing at?" I asked, setting a glass of water and a few pain relievers by the bed for the next morning, along with a hydration drink.

"You're so cute. I want to kiss you."

Oh. "I'm not sure you're in the right frame of mind, Boston."

He sat up and cupped my face. "I might be a bit tipsy, but I know what I want."

"And what is that?"

"Your lips." He leaned forward and pressed his soft lips to mine. I was instantly lost in the connection. Closing my eyes, a moan escaped my mouth.

"That was nice," I said when we parted.

He nodded. "It's too bad, though."

"Too bad about what?"

"Too bad I'm not like you."

Then, after our first kiss, Boston passed out cold.

Chapter Nine
Boston

Going to Chained and imbibing more than my share of alcohol had not been the plan. I wasn't a heavy drinker in general. Usually I was driving or getting home on my own, so even one was a lot. But Elliot had driven, and one drink led to another led to another.

The club was much…so very much. There were people sitting near us wearing different kinds of fetish gear, others in fancy suits, yet others with jeans and crop tops, and a few people even in pajamas. And there was nothing creepy or wrong about any of that. It was just a lot taken all at once, especially knowing that all of them were there because they were into some non-vanilla enjoyment.

I'd gone from my first time playing with a little to sitting in a kink club in a nanosecond, and I handled it poorly—*very* poorly. Drowning in booze was never the answer.

Elliot had taken care of me, though. I owed him…big-time.

Their Little House Boston

I woke up with a headache, two bottles of water by my nightstand, one half gone, and a mouth that tasted like trash. I opened one of the waters and guzzled it, hoping that it would help the headache. Until that happened, I wasn't going to be able to think clearly enough to figure out what bridges I might need to be repair, thanks to my shittastic decision-making the night before. I wasn't even sure how I got to bed; I'd been that bad.

As I tried to piece the whole night together, it slowly came to me. I didn't recall saying anything embarrassing or bad, but that didn't mean I hadn't. I remembered hearing about Elliot's little side and him telling me that he thought I was done for the night. At least I wasn't an asshole when he did that.

I knew how scary that could be, telling someone it was time to be done drinking. I'd had more than my share of altercations trying to be the good friend back in college, but unlike those undergrads, I just went with it. I'd always been a pretty chill drunk, more often falling asleep than anything else. But from agreeing to go home to waking up, it was still all a blur.

I padded into the bathroom to take a long shower. Hydration didn't work by being in humid environments, but I always felt like taking a shower was the starting cure for hangovers, whether it did anything or not. I stayed under the hot water a long time before shampooing my hair and cleaning my body, trying to grasp at memories.

They kept falling away.

And then it hit me.

"Fuck!" I grabbed my cheeks, squeezed them tightly. How—*how* could I have not only told him I liked him but kissed him?

He was little. I was not.

And what did I do? Kissed him like a freaking drunken loser. It probably wasn't even good for him. Drunk kisses were not known as the most caring and sweetest ones on the planet.

I needed to apologize. Maybe he'd be kind enough to forgive me. *Please let that be the case.*

The water started going cold, telling me my shower was done, ready or not. I threw on some clothes and ordered a box of donuts to be delivered from my favorite bakery. I wanted to do something as a thank-you for getting me home/apology gift. Donuts felt like a decent way to go.

I grabbed them off the porch as soon as they arrived and went up to his room, knocking tentatively, worrying that he might be mad at me. He had every right to be.

But when he opened the door, he was smiling.

"You look better than I thought you would."

"I drank too much," I said as I shoved the box of donuts into his arms.

"Yeah. I was there. I remember," He chuckled.

"This is a thank-you for getting me home, and also an apology."

He leaned forward and looked down the hallway, I assumed to see if anybody was coming, then dragged me in, and shut the door behind us. He patted a spot on his bed for me to sit and put the donuts on his dresser before joining me.

"Please don't tell me you're sorry for a kiss." His words were not even close to what I'd expected.

"I am. But it's more than that." I closed my eyes, hating what I had to do but knowing it was for the best. "I'm really new to this little thing, and I-I don't even know if I belong here in this house, if I'm being honest. But you're little. And I like you. A lot. I liked you not drunk. And apparently, I like you a whole lot when I *am*. But also, I'm not a daddy. That I know for sure. And I'm-I'm—"

My apology turned into a full-on babbling session. Before I could finish, his hands were on my cheeks and his lips were on mine. This time, it wasn't a little peck—it was a full-on kiss. Slow and steady at first, and then deeper and deeper until I pulled away, not wanting to push too far but knowing that if we kept going, my hands were going to wander.

"Well, there you go. Now *I* kissed *you*." He grinned.

"That was a revenge kiss?" I asked.

And he pressed his forehead to mine. "No. That's an *I've been wanting to kiss you since we met* kiss."

"You're not mad I might not be little?"

"Why would I be mad at that? Correct me if I'm wrong, but you're new to this and you're trying to figure it out. You *are* trying to figure it out, right?"

"I am," I whispered.

"Why don't you come to Chained with me, and I'll show you the little spaces. Maybe you could check it out."

"Are you sure? It won't be weird after the whole kissing thing?"

He gave me a quick peck. "Not weird at all. Now, tell me about these donuts. You said they're your favorite. Show me which one I need to start with."

Their Little House Boston

    We hadn't figured anything out. Not even close. But, as I bit into my cruller, for the first time since I realized I was attracted to him, I knew that we would.

Chapter Ten

Tripp

After my last trip to Chained, I'd decided not to go for a while, but when several of my friends decided to make an evening of it, I let them talk me into coming. There were often single littles who would like a daddy to play with. The other night there had been several, but they didn't approach me, and I wasn't interested in them anyway. But I'd often found someone more compatible and if not, I'd hang out in the conversation area and visit. Preferable to watching everyone else have fun in the little room while I was alone.

Tonight, there were no special events going on, just an ordinary evening, or as ordinary as things ever got at Chained. Club members were free to come any night, and they could bring guests as long as they got them approved ahead of time. Privacy was very important to many people there, some of whom were quite prominent figures in the local community. In a few cases, they qualified as celebrities, and their membership or even presence there could cause them great damage if it were made public.

Their Little House Boston

I had seen these people there, enjoying the privacy and freedom Chained allowed them. The chance to be themselves away from the cameras and gossip of their daily lives. Even I could appreciate that because my clientele might not understand my private life. Then again, as an insurance guy, I knew a lot about them, and some of their choices were hard for me to grasp. As long as adults treated one another with kindness, though, it was not for me to judge.

The world was full of many people, each of us with our own needs and desires.

I met up with Bridger and the others in the conversation area where they were sharing one of the big/little appetizer platters with their littles. The delicious tidbits helped raise my mood, as did the single whiskey I allowed myself on a night when I was likely to play.

I leaned back on the comfortable leather sofa and listened to daddy talk, my like-minded friends telling amusing stories about both their daddy selves and their day-to-day existence. I was more relaxed than I'd been in a long time when I suddenly spotted the guy who'd been so intriguing to me the other night.

This time, I didn't have to surmise whether he was little. He was with that other guy again. Another little was sitting with him at a table, and they were sipping at sodas and speaking, heads close together. I enjoyed watching them, seeing how the first man seemed to care about his friend, speaking in a soothing tone and patting his hand.

Perhaps it was the second man's first time here? He certainly looked nervous, and I wondered if they would be going to play later. They'd gone to the trouble to dress, but that made them more unusual. Littles, at least those wearing their little clothes, generally went straight to the little room, unless they were accompanied by their daddies like Hudson with Bridger and Austen who was here with his daddy, Clark.

These two continued to talk for a few minutes while sipping their drinks. Their serious expressions made me think they were not in little headspace, yet, and it also had me turning away. Despite being intrigued, I didn't want them to feel uncomfortable because I was staring. It would be unkind, and littles on their own were particularly vulnerable.

Although I was attempting to focus on the conversation at the table, and I wasn't looking directly at them, I couldn't help but notice when they walked past us in the direction of the hallway leading to the little room.

"So, are you busy at this time of year?" Clark asked. "I always imagine insurance to be something people are interested in buying during the darker months. It's just so beautiful out there, now."

"It's not totally predictable, and I haven't made a study of it or looked up the statistics, I think summer is the quietest time. At least for me. Open enrollment in the late fall is a busy time for health insurance, but the other types vary a little more." Littles and insurance, my best topics.

We all chatted for a few more minutes while the littles demolished the little side of the tray and half of the big part. Hudson fell over on his back, patting his stomach. "Daddy, I think I ate too much."

Bridger studied his face. "My poor boy. Do you want to go home and rest?"

He popped up, scrambling to his feet. "No, I'm okay. I was just kidding."

"Crying wolf," his daddy intoned. "I think maybe we should go home, just in case you really are a little sickie."

"No, please," Hudson whined. "I'm all better now. Can't we go to the little room just for a while?"

"You are for sure okay?"

"I'm better now." He grabbed his daddy's hand. "But we'd better play now just in case."

"All right, my best boy." Bridger stood up and allowed his little to tow him away. "Anyone else coming?"

It seemed they all were, and I let the flow of the crowd take me along with them into the little room.

"Maybe you'll find someone to play with this time," Bridger said when I caught up with them.

"You never can tell."

Chapter Eleven
Elliot

"Do you like to paint?" I asked Boston. "I like to paint the pictures by numbers. Those are my favorite." The numbers took the thinking out of it. Once, I tried coloring books as a way to have some fun by myself, but I ended up criticizing my choices of colors and tones. Wasn't so fun in the end.

"Um, yes. I like that too but there are too many people there. I think...I don't know if I want to stay." Boston tugged at his T-shirt and fiddled with the yellow laces on his shoes.

At first, he'd been fine. We read books and played with a light-up board where we could use pegs to make a picture, but that didn't last long. Boston was squirmy and kept shoving his hands into his pockets and rocking on his feet.

There was nervous and then there was glassy-eyed, disassociation. Boston looked like he was experiencing the latter.

Maybe this was too much for him. We should've stuck to the playroom at the little house. Shoot! The last thing I wanted to do was make him uneasy.

I scrambled over solutions in my mind. I didn't quite know how to help him. He looked so cute in his shirt and tiny shorts. There had to be a way to make him more comfortable.

Maybe there was an available daddy.

I scanned the room for someone. Daddies hung out along the edges of the room, waiting for someone to invite them to play.

I spotted one. He was with another little, but I knew for a fact that little had a daddy. In fact, his daddy was across the room, gathering supplies for whatever project they were working on.

The dark-haired daddy might be a third wheel. Maybe he would be interested in playing with us.

There were lots of activities set up tonight. Boston might be interested in one more than the one I'd picked. Maybe he was just going along to get to play with me.

One way to find out.

"See that daddy over there? The one with the dark hair?" I sat next to Boston, putting no distance between our bodies, hoping my nearness would help calm him.

Boston barely looked up but nodded. "He doesn't look mean."

"I bet he's not. I haven't met a mean daddy at Chained. I think they vet most people before they become members."

"What about him?" He used his fingernails to pick at the cotton of his shorts.

"I thought he might like to play with us. I sometimes feel safer when there's a daddy with us."

Boston didn't seem so sure. He wrapped his arm around mine and leaned his head on my shoulder. "Do you think he's nice?"

"We can ask him."

My new friend looked back toward the daddy in question and then back at me. "He does look nice. You go. Ask him. Please."

That was what we were missing. I should've figured. We were missing a daddy. I got up and walked over to the man and waited until he looked at me. I was starstruck. He was handsome from afar, but up close—his attractiveness was breathtaking.

"Can I help you?" he asked.

"It's Elliot," I answered.

"Elliot. Is there something I can do for you?"

I took a long, cleansing breath. "I was wondering if you wanted to play with me and my friend Boston."

"Well, my name is Tripp."

"Daddy Tripp, will you play with us?" I hated asking twice, but I wanted Boston to be comfortable and have some fun—more fun than we'd been having already.

"I would love to play with the two of you. Are you sure your friend wants to join?"

Over my shoulder, I saw Boston getting more antsy by the moment. "Yes."

"Hmm. Okay, but if you or he gets uncomfortable, please let me know."

I nodded. Daddy Tripp got up and ironed the thighs of his pants with his palm. The music grew louder right as the lighting changed. We couldn't hear it all in the playroom, but the switch in bass beats told me they were ramping up the energy.

I tugged on Daddy Tripp's shirt and leaned in. "There's something I have to tell you first. Before we play."

"What is it?" The daddy, tall and a bit muscular, leaned down. His cologne caught my nose, and I inhaled deeply, loving the rich, musky oak and sandalwood. Those scents called to me.

"My friend Boston, well, it's his first time being a little here. In the playroom. We play at home but not here. He's very nervous and shy. I thought a daddy might help calm the situation."

"You're a very good friend, Elliot. It's nice of you to care for others. Are there activities he doesn't want to do? How can I help?"

I shrugged. "I don't think so. Just being there should be enough. We thought you looked like a caring daddy."

"I strive to be. Let's go over there, and you can introduce us. How does that sound?"

Nodding, I took his hand. "That sounds great."

We walked over, and Boston stood up, dusting off his bottom from where he sat on the floor.

"Hello, Boston."

"Boston, this is Daddy Tripp. Daddy Tripp, this is my friend Boston."

"What great names the both of you have," Tripp said.

"Thank you," Boston muttered. "It's like the city."

"It is. I love that."

Chapter Twelve

Tripp

They invited me to join them.

The two littles who had so intrigued me were playing together in the little room. I spotted them the moment I entered, and although I did not approach them, I wished I could. One of the most important elements of the daddy/little culture here at Chained was that the littles should always feel safe. And that meant there was an unspoken rule that said a daddy could not initiate contact—the little had to do it. It was anything but a perfect system because, of course, a little did not want to be rejected, so they were looking for signals that the daddy was interested.

On a good night, that could be entertaining. I'd seen daddies make the funniest faces trying to catch a little's attention without seeming pushy, and littles fall over in giggles at their antics. And I had generally had good luck in finding play partners when I wanted one over the past several years. If a little did not return my interest, no big deal. I wasn't looking for more than an evening's play anyway.

But now? With these two who seemed perfectly content to play together without needing a daddy? I had the awful experience of watching no fewer than three daddies going through the gyrations of letting them know they were available and being ignored before the two looked over at me with interest.

And my heart rate kicked up.

Elliot, the little I'd seen the other night, informed me that this was his friend's first outing as a little, and that he was not very sure of himself. Understood. If Boston had a bad experience, it could make him reluctant to explore an important part of him. Something no daddy would ever want to be responsible for.

"I see there are a lot of fun activities tonight," I said, leaving the choices to them, as they should be. "Anything special you'd like to try?"

The two of them shared a glance then Elliot pointed, and if I hadn't been so happy for the opportunity to spend time with them, my heart would have sunk to my toes.

"Ah, the glitter station." To be fair, glitter was not available every night. Probably not every week, but I seemed to be good at hitting the nights it was. "Lead the way, boys!"

We had to wait a few minutes, since the table was popular, but as soon as two seats opened, I pulled them out and helped them to sit down. A nice lady with a big smile, introduced herself to them as Miss Rebecca, and helped them to get started on the project, creating a sparkly picture frame for "a picture of your favorite stuffie or maybe a pet."

"I don't have a pet," Elliot told her, shaking his head sadly.

Boston offered a shrug but no words. It was enough to understand he didn't have one either. Little boys should have an animal to play with. Juno would love them. Sometimes I felt like I wasn't enough fun for her but these two...

"Do you like dogs?"

Boston looked up from where he was gripping a bottle of glue in one hand, a five-by-seven frame in the other. His eyes held such longing, my breath stalled. "You have a dog?"

"I'll show you." I automatically reached for my phone in my pocket, only to remember that my phone and all its photos were safely locked up until I was ready to leave. "That is, yes, I do."

"Is it a big one?" asked a third little from the same table. "My dog is giant, and I am going to put his picture in the frame when I get home."

"Will it fit in the frame?" Elliot asked, a frown creasing his brow. "Maybe you should ask for a bigger one."

"Miss Rebecca," the little said, "I need a frame this big." His arms stretched wide. "Or my fluffy dog-dog Bruce won't fit."

The staffer's eyes twinkled. "Well, I don't have one that big, but maybe your daddy will print out a photo the right size."

"My daddy can do that," he bragged. "He can do anything."

"Here's the biggest we have, just so he doesn't have to work any harder than necessary," Miss Rebecca said, handing him what was probably eight by ten. "Now, what color is your dog-dog? You'll want to pick out the best glitter to make his fur shine."

"I can't get any glitter on him, though. I'm not even allowed to pet him after I do art until Daddy baths me."

A very good policy in my mind. Getting glitter out of the fur of a gigantic fluffy dog...not a job any daddy wanted. Sounded like this little shared a dog and a life with his daddy, and as he and Elliot and Boston completed their projects, he confirmed that. It was a happy picture, and my imagination jumped to what it would be like to come home to dinner with these two. They'd be throwing a ball for Juno while I grilled up some burgers or hot dogs, then it would be bath time. My giant tub had been more of an asset than I realized when I bought the place.

They would both fit, along with lots of bath toys.

I shook myself free of the thought, surprised I'd done such future tripping. We'd just met, done one scene—which was very much still happening—and they might not be nearly as interested in seeing me again as I was them.

After glitter, we did paint and the night's floor puzzle and wound up with a story. I walked them to the group changing room, bemused by the unusual connection I could see between the littles. Two boys who obviously were attracted to one another in friendship but more. Maybe they just wanted a daddy for the evening. Boston was very new to the scene.

But no matter what, even if it didn't come to anything, I wanted to get to know them better. So before I left, I gave them my business card. "My cell phone number is on there. I'd like to see you both again, maybe for dinner, if you are interested."

"Thank you." Elliot took the card and held onto it. Not a yes or a no. Most likely they needed to talk. As they disappeared into the room, they left a trail of glitter from their completed frames. I wondered what picture they'd put in them, since they had no pets. Probably a stuffie. But what kind?

Chapter Thirteen

Elliot

I kept the business card on my nightstand that night and tucked it into my pocket—kept it with me for a day or so while life was busy and work made me almost forget about it.

Almost.

Tripp had been so loving and thoughtful. He was patient with Boston. Never pushy in the least. He watched over us as we painted and put together the puzzle.

If he noticed the attraction I felt to Boston, he didn't say so. Even when we wanted to make a glitter frame, he didn't bat an eye. Some daddies didn't like glitter. It was a mess at times but sooo much fun.

Boston didn't say a word about calling the daddy, but I wanted to.

By the second day, the card was burning a hole in my pocket, begging me to pay attention.

While on my lunch hour, which was six at night since I was working the afternoon shift, I went outside to the reading garden and called the number. The place was usually busy during the day. Kids reading and soaking up the sun. Moms and dads letting their babies get some sun and a bit of quiet. Friends having coffee while discussing their favorite new reads amongst the seasonal flowers.

"Hello?" Tripp's voice instantly made my body shudder in the best way.

"Hello, this is Elliot. I don't know if you remember me? From Chained."

His chuckle wrapped around my torso, warming me. "Of course, I remember you, Elliot. I'm so glad you called."

"I'm at work. On my lunch break."

"Hmm. Where do you work? I hear some car sounds but also a few birds."

My turn to laugh. "I am a librarian. I'm outside in the reading garden, hence the birds, but also, we are near a busy intersection."

"A librarian. That sounds like an interesting job."

We talked for a while about my job, and he asked me if I was having something decent to eat on my break.

"Leftover bowtie pasta. Sometimes, at the house, we make big meals, and everyone can have a portion or as much as they want."

"That's good to hear." I heard him click something like a remote. Perhaps he was turning the TV off so he could hear me better. "I hope to get to know you and Boston better."

"I want to get to know you, too. Where do you work?" A dog barked in the background.

"Hold on, please, Elliot. I have a package. One second. Please don't hang up."

While I was on hold, I took a few bites of food, but I was way more interested in talking than eating.

Tripp came back on the phone. "Sorry about that."

"You have a dog?"

"I do. Her name is Juno. I adopted her from a shelter."

"Is she big?" I asked.

"She is. Do you like dogs?"

For a few minutes, we talked about dogs. He told me he owned an insurance agency, giving him some freedom to make his own work hours, although they were often long anyway.

"You and Boston are friends?" Tripp asked. I was wondering if he noticed the budding care between us. Maybe he did.

"We are."

"But you and he are more than friends, right?"

Were we? "I don't know."

"I can see you like him. It's sweet the way you two look at each other. Speak to one another."

"I like him a lot, but..."

"And I like both of you, but I think you two should figure out how you feel about each other before anything else."

"Anything else?"

He chuckled again. The sound did things to me.

I checked my watch. Shoot. My lunch was almost over.

"I would love to take you and Boston on a date, Elliot."

"I would like that too."

"How about you and Boston figure out where you are and then call me."

"I would really like to go on a date with you but also with him. This is confusing."

"It's okay. Take your time. I'm a patient man. Call me when you can, even if nothing is decided. Your voice is soothing to me, sweet one."

His calmed me. Also, his presence. His kindness and the umbrella of security he gave Boston made him all that more attractive.

"Okay. Goodbye, Tripp."

"Good night, Elliot."

I hung up more bewildered than ever. I wanted a daddy like Tripp, but I also had an undeniable tether to Boston. He and I really needed to have a talk.

I kept myself busy for the rest of the night, trying and failing to keep my mind off my predicament. Nothing worked. I didn't even take my break. I was a bit hungry, but my nerves were getting the best of me and taking most of that away.

When I got back to the house, I made a beeline for Boston's room. There was a chance he was fast asleep, but I knocked anyway.

He wasn't asleep. "Hey, can we talk?"

Chapter Fourteen

Boston

I couldn't get Daddy Tripp out of my head. But also, I couldn't get Elliot out of my head. It was flooded with men and all things little and daddy, and I wasn't sure what to do with all of that.

I'd never considered myself poly, but also never thought to myself, I wasn't. My relationships in the past had always been fairly short, never getting too serious. Between work or just not meshing, I never ventured there with anyone.

But the more I thought about these two men, the more I wondered if maybe the three of us could work together. Monroe had mentioned once in passing that my room had previously belonged to a little who was now living with his daddy and another little. So it wasn't unheard of to share.

He never said they were in love or anything more than doing scenes, but moving in together felt like a pretty big commitment. I couldn't imagine a scenario where it was just playing together once in a while.

I swapped out my crayon for a different shade of blue and went back to my coloring page. My head had been buzzing all day, and I hoped being in the playroom might help with that. I supposed it did, in a small way, but only enough for me to try and process what my emotions and desires were going through, not enough to silence it.

"You're going to break the crayon if you keep grabbing it that hard."

I hadn't heard Elliot come in, but he was now standing beside me and correct. I not only would break it; I had already done so. Four broken crayons sat beside the box. I put new ones on my mental list of things to buy. These were communal supplies, and it was only right to replace what I damaged.

"Yeah, I have a lot on my mind."

He sat across from me, snagging a crayon of his own. "Can I help?"

I nodded, unsure if he meant with the picture or my confusion. I was happy with either or both.

"Are you thinking about Daddy Tripp?"

"I-I was. And I was thinking about you. And I was thinking about whether or not I was little. And about whether or not I was poly. And just—a lot of things." It all came out, much easier than I'd expected.

I loved the way I could share with him. Not once did I feel uncomfortable about being open with him, not after the kiss apology, anyway. He wouldn't judge me. Or, if he did, he wouldn't make me feel bad about it. Judging kind of comes with being human. It's how you react to those feelings that matters.

He continued coloring as he asked questions to clarify the different things I was feeling when needed, but never pushing or ignoring me to make the bicycle he was coloring extra pretty. He was giving me the sense of…privacy, as I let it all out.

And when I was done, he put the crayon back in the box and his hand on mine.

"Let's go to my room." It wasn't a question. He stood up, holding my hand. "We'll clean up later." He must have sensed my hesitation.

"Sometimes, you seem like Daddy." I meant it as an inside thought, but it didn't stay there.

"Yeah, that's one of the things we should probably talk about." He intertwined our fingers, and we wandered back to his room, where we both sat on his bed, facing each other, criss-cross applesauce.

"I have Daddy Tripp's number. And I talked to him the other day. He said he's interested in dating both of us. Is that something you'd consider?"

Their Little House Boston

I nearly bounced on the bed. I thought wanting both of them was asking for too much and that I'd end up with neither. And here he was saying the door was open, that it was a possibility.

"I'd like to try. I didn't get jealous when you two were playing together." I wasn't gonna put it past me that I might at some point feel that way, but initial gut reactions were pretty telling in my experience.

He took both my hands in his and held them between us.

"Now, about what you said about me being Daddy. I don't know what it means either. But from the first time I met you, I liked taking care of you. But also—I need a daddy."

"I don't understand what you mean." I was nervous that he was about to reject me. Only he didn't.

"It means, if we do this, and we start dating Daddy Tripp, I'd want him to be Daddy. But that doesn't mean I wouldn't want to take care of you too. And I have no idea what that would look like. But if that's okay with you, then maybe we can move on from here. Maybe start with a date where we can figure out if we even like each other outside of Chained."

"Okay." There was more to say, but I couldn't find the words, so I remained silent.

"Who knows? Maybe Daddy Tripp's kind of a jerk when he's in other places."

I rolled my eyes. "He seemed like a nice daddy to me."

"Me, too. But we won't know unless we get to know him better. Should I call him?"

"Yeah. I'd like that." Having Elliot take care of things made this a whole lot easier. "You know what else I'd like?"

"No, but I bet you're gonna tell me, sweet boy."

Something about the way he said sweet boy warmed me up from the inside.

"I'd like if I could kiss you."

"Nope. I wanna kiss you." He took our joined hands, pulled me to him, and sealed his lips to mine.

We stayed in his room, kissing on his bed for a real long time, not going any further, just enjoying the taste of each other, the feel of our bodies close together.

It was nice. Really nice.

I couldn't help but wonder if it would feel this good once we had a third. I was both thrilled and terrified to find out.

Chapter Fifteen

Tripp

After my conversation with Elliot, I wasn't sure things were going to go any further, but to my surprise, a little while later, my phone rang again. Elliot said they had talked about me and decided they wanted to have dinner with me.

I had by no means been sure that would happen, but now that it had, I knew exactly where I wanted to take them. Somewhere we could enjoy delicious food and quiet conversation in a nice atmosphere. I texted my reservation right away and received confirmation. Although I'd spent a good many evenings there wining and dining clients, The Golden Buffalo was busy enough I'd been slightly concerned about them having the availability I wanted.

Elliot and Boston arrived at the Buffalo in a rideshare. I'd offered to pick them up, but they declined, saying they didn't want me to go out of my way, since I'd be coming right from my office. The address was on the card I gave them, so they knew the restaurant was just a couple of blocks from the agency. But also, they were using good sense, meeting someone they'd only known for a few hours, member of Chained or not. Once we'd spent some time together, they could decide whether to get in a car alone with me.

I waited for them in the bar, sipping a whiskey and people watching. Most of the others were from the surrounding offices, having after-work drinks with coworkers or client meetings, but in an hour or two, they'd all be gone, replaced by couples and others there for a nice meal in comfortably elegant surroundings.

"Mr. Stanz?" The hostess approached me. "Your table is ready whenever your guests arrive."

"Thank you, Ariana. I was a little early, but they should be here any moment." Provided they hadn't changed their minds. I checked my watch. "Due in five minutes."

"Just let me know." She lifted her hand in a wave and headed back toward the front where her station lay. But no less than a minute later, she returned, leading Boston and Elliot into the bar. "Mr. Stanz. Your guests are here."

"Then I guess we'd better go to our table, unless you'd both like to stay in the bar for a while?" Which wouldn't be great considering the dining arrangements, but it seemed polite not to rush them. "We can order cocktails at our table as well."

They exchanged a glance, something I'd noticed they often did. "I think the table is good," Elliot said.

Boston nodded, and our hostess turned on a heel and started through the dining room. "Right this way, gentlemen."

Our table was located in a private room tucked away behind the main one, something I had used a few times for business but never for personal evenings. Once our server came in and took drink orders and left, Boston and Elliot picked up their menus, but they both seemed a little twitchy. Maybe they thought I had some kind of nefarious plan?

"I reserved the room so we'd have quiet to talk without worrying about people at the next table listening in, although the servers are going back and forth right outside the door, and of course coming in and out," I said, wanting to get rid of any concerns. "But if you'd rather we eat out there, we can. Whatever you'd prefer."

"No, this is nice." Boston smiled shyly. "I've never been in a private dining room in a restaurant. Is the food the same?"

"Unless you place a special order, but I thought we'd just choose from the menu, since I don't know what you like best. Everything is good, though."

"Lots of people think littles only eat macaroni and cheese or nuggies," Elliot said, "and, true, when I am in little headspace, I often do enjoy that sort of cuisine, but when I'm big, I love seafood."

"The Buffalo, in addition to all the red meat their name implies, has a whole page of seafood in the menu, and I've tried most of it and never been disappointed. Boston, what is your preference?"

"Just chicken, maybe."

"That sounds good," Elliot echoed him, setting the menu down.

Oh, heck no, we weren't playing the *get the cheapest thing because it's all I deserve* game tonight. "Really?" I allowed disappointment to color my tones. "That makes me uncomfortable to get what I wanted to. But the chicken is fine."

"No, don't do that," Boston protested. "We don't want you not to get...what were you thinking of?"

We all had bison filet and lobster tail. And it did my heart good to see the two of them enjoying their food. We chatted easily throughout dinner about work and the news and the weather, just first-date stuff, but as the server set the slice of cookie monster cheesecake on the table.

"I didn't even know they served this here," I marveled, eyeing the blue filling and multiple kinds of cookies in the crust and as decorations. "What is it exactly?"

"Cookies-and-cream cheesecake with food coloring for effect and a layer of ganache and all the cookies." Elliot was well-informed, but Boston simply stared at it and licked his lips.

"Wow." I used my fork to break off a small taste. "It's good?"

"Delicious!" Elliot scooped some up, followed by Boston, and they touched forks before giving me a glance.

I held out mine and as one, we put them in our mouths and chewed.

"Well?" Elliot looked from me to Boston and back again. "Good?"

"Delicious." Boston went back in for another bite. "Best dessert ever."

"How did you even know to ask for it?" I also took some more. "It wasn't on the menu."

"It's pretty popular on social media," Elliot replied. "And after a perfect dinner, I thought it was worth asking at least."

The ending to our meal provided the perfect little-ish touch to the evening, even if we did have it with espressos. And over our shared blue cheesecake, we decided to take things as they came. No pressure, get to know one another and see how it went.

For a first date, it was pretty darn awesome, and when they let me drive them home, I walked them to their door and gave each a sweet kiss good night.

Chapter Sixteen

Boston

I'd been so nervous about dinner. It was a meal at a restaurant, a typical date in that respect. But I was going with two men that I liked, and we were trying out having a three-relationship of some sort between us. That, in and of itself, was so new to me. So much of this was—especially knowing he was a daddy and, the first time he saw me, I was dressed in my boyfriend's little clothes at a sex club.

And then there was the fact that I kept thinking about Elliot as my boyfriend. Was he? No. But he wasn't my friend either. He was more.

It was a lot to take in, and my head was really bad at shutting down when I needed it to.

I hadn't needed to worry at all. From the time we climbed out of our rideshare and met Tripp at the restaurant, everything had been wonderful. I felt comfortable and safe. The food was amazing, and, even though I didn't understand how any of this would work, I left the restaurant knowing that I wanted it to and feeling like the same was true for the other two men at my side.

Tripp walked us up to the door and kissed us goodbye so sweetly, I nearly melted. If we'd lived somewhere else, I'd have invited him in. But this was a little house, bringing a daddy in without notice wasn't acceptable, and it was probably for the best. It kept us from going too fast, too soon.

Or so I thought.

Elliot and I both walked up the stairs toward our rooms, but as we reached the landing, I knew I wasn't ready to say good night.

"Can I have a sleepover?" I asked, meaning just that...sleeping over to sleep.

"Sure. Do you want to grab Koalakins?"

"Yeah. I'll meet you back here. I'll take a quick shower too." It would give me time to get my longing to kiss him under control, because tonight, that urge was so much stronger than in the past, and I'd want it to go well beyond that. This was complicated enough without adding sex to the mix before we figured things out.

We agreed to meet in thirty, and I went to my room, pulled out a pair of my favorite comfy jams, and popped into the shower.

My initial thought was that I would take matters into my own hands. It wouldn't take much to reach down, grab my cock, and jerk the arousal away.

Only it felt wrong—like I was being disrespectful in some way. And I knew that was ridiculous. Neither man would fault me for taking care of myself. Heck, they'd probably think it was hot, knowing I did it thinking about them.

But still, I couldn't bring myself to do so and left the shower just as needy and horny as I was when I got in.

Koalakins and my pillow in hand, I headed down to Elliot's room and walked inside. I should have knocked. Of course I should have. It was the polite thing to do. But I hadn't thought of it at the time, and, when I stepped inside, he was standing there, buck naked, his cock semihard, just out there in the open as he toweled off his hair.

"I-I'm sorry. Do you want me to leave?"

He shook his head. "Nah, you're good."

I quickly shut the door behind me, not wanting anybody else to see his naked glory. Once I did, I didn't even pretend to hide how I felt about seeing him. I raked my eyes up and down his body, soaking in his form.

"Is it okay? Can I?" I asked, and he looked back at me quizzically. "I want a taste. Can I have a taste?"

He swallowed before giving a slight nod.

I threw my pillow and Koalakins on the bed behind him and dropped to my knees. This was going to be fabulous. I hadn't even touched him yet, and he was already getting harder, just knowing what I longed to do with him.

"Thank you. I need a snack." I put my hand behind him, holding him steady, my fingers grabbing his ass, and took my hand and wrapped it around his hardening length. He was mostly hard already in anticipation. It was so fucking hot.

I jerked him a few times as I circled his tip with my tongue, and then I took him into my mouth, reaching behind him with my other hand and pulling him toward me so that he went all the way to the back of my throat with one quick motion.

He groaned—and that only spurred me on.

There was a time and place for teasing and coaxing and playing. This wasn't it. More than anything, I wanted him to come fast and hard...to see the magic I could do, with none of the torture that we'd probably both have been facing being so close to

Daddy Tripp at dinner and neither of us being able to do anything about it.

I worked his cock like it was my job—taking him back as far as I could, swallowing, twirling my tongue, holding him firm as I fucked him with my mouth until his body froze and the warmth of his cum shot to the back of my throat.

I made sure not to lose a drop, swallowing it all and savoring the taste. I licked him clean before I pulled off of him.

"Oh my fucking god. You know what you're doing." His fingers were woven through my hair, holding on tightly. I'd been so into what I was doing I hadn't even noticed him grabbing on.

He let go, and I stumbled back until I was sitting on the bed. I licked my lips, looked back at him, wanting him to see how much this sated me. I didn't even care that I was hard as a rock. This...this was enough.

I crawled into the bed behind him, snuggling for the night.

"Probably put some pajamas on before you go to sleep," I teased. "You'll get cold." I'd have preferred he be naked, but the room was chilly, and if I could take care of him in that small way, then I wanted to do so.

Their Little House Boston

It struck me that my Koalakins was sitting here, while we were in a little house, having just eaten dinner with a daddy, but everything about what we'd just done was just typical dating fun. Hotter than, because Elliot, but nothing kinky or little about it.

I didn't feel like he was being a daddy, or that either one of us had any role other than two guys who liked each other trying to get off.

I closed my eyes, using Koalakins partly as a pillow, partly as a snuggly, as Elliot shuffled around the room getting ready for bed. I hadn't expected the covers to be pulled off me or for me to find him kneeling between my legs, licking his lips as his gaze met mine. The man was hungry with a capital H, and I was there for it.

"My turn," he said—like I could deny him that.

I raised my hips to help him pull my pajama pants down and then watched as he lowered his mouth onto my cock. Unlike me, he did take his time—licking, sucking, nibbling, stroking.

If he thought I was good at this, he was a freaking prodigy.

Chapter Seventeen
Elliot

As soon as I caught my breath and got dressed again, the guilt settled like a boulder on my chest.

"What is it?" Boston asked, turning over to face me.

"It doesn't feel right without Tripp."

"Yeah…" He looked as torn as I felt. All of us together, well, that was the reason we were so hot and bothered we couldn't take the tension anymore.

"What should we do?" I asked my friend. No, friend wasn't right. What we had was clearly more than that.

"Should we call him and tell him? It feels like we just cheated on him, but we didn't. I don't know." Boston was right.

"I think we should. Do you think he's home yet?"

"Let's call him. If he answers, then we'll know."

"If he's driving, he won't answer," I reminded him. "Remember, he said he never talks or texts when behind the wheel." No true daddy ever would.

I picked up my phone, though, and we called him. He answered on the first ring, saying he'd just gotten home. What great timing we had.

"Can we video chat with you?" I asked.

"Of course. Let me get settled, and I'll call you."

Boston put his clothes back on, and we sat on the bed, our backs against the headboard. While we waited, Boston reached over and threaded his fingers with mine. It was the first time we'd held hands, and it meant everything to me. We were together. Also in a throuple or whatever we were called, but we were together.

The phone rang, and I entered the video chat, making sure we both were in the frame.

"I'm glad to hear from you so soon after our date. Is everything okay?"

"We need to tell you something," Boston blurted out. I was glad for it. I was going to work up to the admission, but there it was.

"Please do. You can tell me anything."

Boston looked to me. Oh, now he was shy. "We were very worked up after you left, and we had sex. Not really sex, but..."

"I see. Did you enjoy yourselves?"

"We did," Boston said, tightening his hold on my hand.

"I'm glad you two were honest with me, but I'm also happy you had a good time. I'd like for you to tell me what you did. It really turns me on thinking about the two of you together."

It did? I thought he would be upset. I should've known better. Tripp was a patient and gentle daddy.

"We gave each other blow jobs," I said. No point in dancing around the fact.

"Hmm, I think since I wasn't there, I should get some details. Don't you?"

Boston gasped. "Yes, Daddy."

"Good. Tell me exactly what you did. I'm getting hard already. Tell me how you two took care of each other."

We told him in detail how we sucked on each other's cocks and made each other come. While we did, Tripp showed us how we were affecting him and how he was taking care of himself while we watched.

I'd never had a sexy video chat before, if this counted as that. I didn't know the rules in that regard. I'd never been with anyone I trusted enough to even talk about this kind of thing through a device that could record before. And now I was with two men who I trusted completely with keeping this private.

Daddy Tripp wasn't embarrassed at all about his arousal at our story and in return, I tried to make sure to leave no detail untold. Boston wasn't quite as open, and I wasn't sure if it was due to shyness or because he was so busy watching our daddy stroking his very impressive member. He was long, thick, and my mouth watered just from looking at it.

If I'd been in the room with him, I'd have been begging for a taste, but I wasn't. That would have to wait until the next time I saw him.

He came, loudly, our names on his lips. It was the hottest thing I'd ever seen, and it was going to take a large spot in my spank bank, for sure.

Daddy said good night, so he could go and clean up, leaving only Boston and me in my bed.

"We should sleep." I climbed off the bed to turn off the overhead light and then got back in bed with Boston. He threw his arm over me and snuggled in close. "Miss me?"

"Yesssss." He kissed my shoulder. "You were gone for at least ten seconds. Do you think Daddy Tripp misses us?"

"How could he not, after we made him come like that?"

"That was hot." His leg wrapped around mine as if holding me there. "I'd never seen someone I know do that before. I didn't know I liked it."

"I didn't know it was my thing, either. It's fun to learn new things about ourselves, isn't it?" I was speaking to him but also to myself. I'd sort of thought I had my preferences in the bedroom all figured out, but since these two men entered my life, I was no longer sure.

"Especially when I'm figuring it out with—" He was cut off by his own yawn.

"Go to sleep, Boston. Love you." I hadn't meant to say it, but it felt right and there was no way I was pulling it back.

"Love you, too. Night."

He said it back. Boston. Said. It. Back. Best night ever.

Chapter Eighteen

Tripp

After our first date, we'd had several more. The three of us went to dinner at other, more casual places that each mentioned liking, and one night we went to the movies. So far, our time together had been "big" time, which I was enjoying very much. We were not on a schedule, and every opportunity to spend time with Boston and Elliot was one I would not have missed. But, one night while sitting outside an ice cream shop, the two of them licking cones in a disturbingly sexy way while I sipped a root beer float, a topic came up that we'd so far avoided.

"I think it's time for us to try dating one on one."

Boston's cheeks reddened. "We did sort of do that that one night, Elliot and me."

"Yes, you did." The three of us were still at the kissing-good-night stage, and other than that one evening, they had not repeated their intimacy. Even though I had told them I was very glad they had a good time together and never tried to discourage them because I didn't have the right to.

Which was why I had plans tonight with just Elliot. The night of the ice cream date, we'd agreed that it was important that each of us have an individual relationship with each of the others. I'd never imagined myself in a three-way relationship, and I was navigating with care, not wanting to make any mistakes so big that I could not correct them.

And, while I loved spending time with the pair, enjoying their interactions, I had to admit I looked forward to an evening with Elliot. He had an outspokenness that often had him speaking for both of them, and it should be interesting to converse just with him. With that in mind, I'd planned an evening conducive to conversation.

Somewhere we could talk without interruption and establish a connection with just the two of us. I didn't want to go the private dining room at The Golden Buffalo for this date, since it really was a place where we'd created a memory for the three of us. After considering and rejecting a number of other ideas, I sent him a text. *Do you like horse riding?*

The reply came in about two seconds. And it consisted of a long series of hearts. So, yes to horse riding.

My next text was to a friend, another daddy who while a member of Chained, lived far enough away on his ranch to make it in rarely. When he confirmed that we were welcome to come for the afternoon I had in mind, I let Elliot know to be ready the next afternoon. Then I went to work on our picnic.

"Where are we going, Tripp?" he asked when we were in the car, headed out of town. "I haven't been horse riding since I was a kid. My uncle took me to the stables in the park a couple of times, but we aren't headed in that direction."

"No, not the park. We are visiting my friend's ranch. He invited us to come and ride as long as we like, and I thought we could have a picnic."

"Horse riding and a picnic?" He grinned over at me, looking as simply happy as I'd ever seen him. "What a perfect date."

We had about an hour-and-a-half drive, which also fell in with my plan to spend time talking, and being together, but Elliot was so excited about our trip we mostly spoke about horses. I had more experience than he did, had summered on a ranch a few times as a teen, working, but Elliot's enthusiasm had me every bit as excited as he was. I told him about what it was like working on the ranch. It had been a seminal experience for a city kid, and while I hadn't chosen to do that work forever, I'd never forget it.

"You're not only a daddy, you're a cowboy daddy."

"Well, mostly I fixed fences, but I do like that image." I turned off the highway and drove under the Triple L Ranch sign then down a long dirt road. "My friend is going to be away this afternoon, but he told us to go right to the stables and his ranch manager will set us up."

"Okay." He didn't say anything else until we entered the white building with its row of stalls, some empty, others with horses peering over the doors to see who had come to visit them. "Tripp, are horses always this big?"

"No not all." I paused to stroke a velvet nose. "Come see this sweetie, Elliot."

He moved up beside me and reached a tentative hand toward the white mark on the mare's forehead. "What a pretty girl. Is that her name on the door? Star?"

"It sure is." At the voice from behind us, I turned and saw Griffy the ranch manager approaching. "And she's the one we have in mind for you. Elliot, right?"

"Yes. She's tall." Elliot shook his hand, but his eyes held doubt. "I don't have a lot of experience."

"Miss Star is gentle as a lamb. You'll be safe as houses on her back."

As we rode out of the barn, Elliot asked me in a quiet voice, "What does safe as houses mean?"

"I know it's a British expression, and Griffy is from Montana. I think it just means really safe. How are you doing with her?"

"So far, okay," he said, letting go of the reins with one hand to stroke his horse's neck. "Thank you for this. It's a dream come true."

We rode for about an hour before we reached the meadow I had in mind for our picnic. I climbed off the gelding I rode and helped Elliot down. He moved a little stiffly, so we walked around for a few minutes before I spread out the blanket and picnic on the soft grasses and settled in to eat and continue to talk. It was like catching up with an old friend from a previous life who wanted to know what I'd been doing in this one.

And when the last sandwich was gone, the apples all crunched, we lay back side by side and held hands, gazing up at the sky and watching the big puffy clouds blow by. And then, Elliot rested his head on my shoulder and fell asleep. It was a perfect spot for a romantic assignation, but I didn't want to make love with just one of them for the first time together. Nothing wrong with their one-time evening or even if they chose to do it again. It was just what I wanted and needed—both of them at once.

The horses grazed on the lush grass, and I lay quietly while Elliot slept. It was such a sign of trust to sleep around another person, or at least that was how I'd always felt, and I felt so honored.

Finally, the sun was getting low and though I hated to do it, I woke my date. "We need to get back before it's dark," I told him, helping him to sit up. "Or I'd let you sleep longer."

"It's okay." He stood and took a couple of steps, groaning. "I think I need to ride more often. I'm all stiff."

"We can do that for sure," I told him. "Let's lead the horses for a few minutes so you loosen up, okay?"

"Okay."

I packed up and picked up my horse's reins then we started down. After ten minutes, we mounted and continued down to the ranch where the manager took the horses and turned them over to hands, refusing to let us do any of the work. "Boss wants you up at the house for dinner," he said. "And I'm not to take no for an answer."

So much for aloneness, but Elliot seemed fine with it. He asked all kinds of questions about ranch life and ate his weight in brisket and apple pie.

Then we drove home, where I walked him to the door for a kiss. The sexual tension vibrated, and we'd get there. When the time was right.

Chapter Nineteen

Boston

Things had been going really well with Elliot, Daddy Tripp, and me. We'd gone out together, all three of us, a few times, and his dog Juno pretty much stole my heart instantly when we met her on video chat.

There was so much cuteness in that ball of fur, I couldn't even stand it. I teased that I wanted him to bring her to our house so I could keep her, knowing full well that A) Tripp would never allow that, and B) we weren't supposed to have pets here. But the idea of snuggling up with her during a movie night sounded pretty fabulous to me.

I checked myself in the mirror one last time before hunting Elliot down. "I need a fit check." I twirled slowly in front of him.

"Yeah, you nailed it. Those are your sexy jeans, and not an eye in the place will be anywhere else."

"Sexy jeans? I didn't know I had sexy jeans? Aren't they all the same?" I knew sexy jeans existed, of course. I could reach into Elliot's drawers and pick his out with ease. But I always thought mine were all the same. Heck, they were even the same brand and style. Guess not, if Elliot liked these. I made note of which they were for future reference.

"Nope. Those cup your ass just right," he said, giving my butt a playful smack. "Tripp gonna be here soon?"

I checked my phone. "Yeah. Next couple minutes."

"Well then, you'd better hurry and kiss me before he gets here. And if you're anywhere with chocolate, don't forget my date tax."

"Date tax?"

"Yes. Date tax. If I can't be there for the cake or the pie or the cookies or the candy or whatever chocolate you are around, you have to bring some back to me. It's only fair."

"And did you bring me back a dessert last time you went out?" He'd brought me nachos, but I was ignoring that, enjoying our light teasing.

"Cheese is just as good," he said with a grin. He wasn't wrong. "Now, kiss me. He'll come exactly on time and you know it."

I gave him a far too brief kiss.

"Did you want to say hello?"

"Nope." He tapped my nose. "This is your date, not mine. And it's a first date for you two without me, so hurry on. I'll wait for my tax."

Another playful smack on my ass, and I jogged down the stairs, opening the door just as Daddy walked up the front steps.

"Little excited for our date?"

My head bobbed up and down like those silly bobbleheads, and I didn't even care. "I am."

I pulled the door shut behind me and hurried into his waiting arms. We'd kissed, held hands, and hugged during our times with all three of us, and we'd had conversations and video chats that went a lot further than that, but there was still a thrill about feeling his arms around me.

"Where are we going?"

"That's for me to know," he said.

He kissed my cheek and took my hand, dragging me to the car as I protested, very poorly, about needing to know where we were going to make sure I was dressed properly.

"You need to trust that if you weren't, I'd have told you by now.

"Because you're a daddy?" I asked.

"I suppose so, yes. But also, because I like you and wouldn't want you to feel uncomfortable."

He liked me. Heart emojis bumped around in my mind.

Tripp opened the passenger door, and I slid inside.

We ended up at karaoke night at a local bar. It wasn't a random date choice. Once, when we were talking about what little things I liked, I'd mentioned once how much fun I had singing silly songs at karaoke. Because, to me, anything silly and fun and not prim and proper felt little at first.

But the more I played and the more I talked to both Elliot and Tripp, the more I realized that there was fun, and then there were the things that helped me forget about the world around me and kind of slip away. And those were little. At least, to me, they were.

Coloring didn't work as well for me, but blocks, cars, and listening to stories did wonders. Crafts, too, as long as they weren't hard. Glue and glitter all day long. But cutting? That brought all the thoughts back as I focused on making sure I didn't mess up the lines. I pretty much avoided that now when I was in the playroom.

Elliot said you never stopped learning about who you were and what you liked. So, yay me.

I ordered soda instead of alcohol, remembering what it was like the time I went to Chained with Elliot. I hadn't done anything I regretted. In a lot of ways, being drunk had helped me say things I needed to, but I had woken up with a horrible headache and missing parts of my memory from the night before. I wanted to remember every single second with Tripp. Soda, it was.

We sang, both together and solo, listened to some really horrible renditions of songs that weren't good in the first place, and heard a few people sing well enough that they should have been on open-mic night and not at a karaoke bar.

There was laughter, a few flinches, and a whole lot of shared food. And when we could no longer take the noise, we went for a walk, finding a little café for dessert…a café where I got a piece of chocolate cake to bring back to Elliot as my date tax. We even kissed under the stars, but all too soon, it was time for me to go home.

I was happy for an evening when I didn't want to say good night instead of one where I wished it were over. Having to endure the company of some dates I'd had in my past was no fun. Reluctance to part from Tripp was a good thing, even if I didn't love it.

Tripp kissed my cheek and whispered, "Be sure to tell Elliot all about our night when you give him this cake," making me once again hate the stupid rule that stated he had to stay outside unless prior arrangements were made.

"I will, Daddy Tripp." It was the first time I'd called him that the entire night. It felt right, and the smile he gave in return reached his eyes before he gave me one last kiss and walked back to his car.

I ran to Elliot's room, not only to give him his date tax but to let him know everything that was happening.

He snatched the box fast and opened it. "I guess I have to keep you." He plopped onto his bed, taking the plastic spork that came with the cake and digging in for a huge bite.

"I left something for you on the dresser." His mouth was full and, if he hadn't indicated the piece of furniture with his head, I might not have understood what he was saying at all.

"For me?" I walked over and found a drawing of Koalakins one of the frames we made the first night with Daddy Tripp at Chained.

"You drew this for me?" It was good...really good.

"Of course I did. You weren't going to use your frame. It required cutting." He chuckled, his mouth still full of food.

"You saw that?" I hadn't mentioned it, but he knew.

"Of course I did. I pay attention."

"Thank you." I wanted to say so much more than that, to tell him how it warmed my heart that he took the time to notice the small things, how it made me feel on top of the world. Instead, I sat beside him and opened my mouth.

"What? Didn't you have your own?"

"No. I had pie." And it had been delicious.

He let out a fake sigh. "Here." He fed me a spork full of cake...his cake. It was the most delicious bite I'd ever eaten.

We devoured the rest of it as I told him all about my night...a night that I wanted to include kissing him breathless. He was very on board with that plan, and we were sure to tell Daddy Tripp all about it, not because he made us but because he thought it was as hot as we did.

Chapter Twenty

Boston

It had been the slowest day of all days in the history of forever. I was sure of it.

Knowing that I was finally going to get to go to Chained with both Daddy Tripp and Elliot resulted in the clock ticking at a snail's pace. Every minute felt like a year. It was worse than waiting for Santa at Christmas as a small child.

One glance at my phone told me that very soon, the slow torture that was being patient would be over.

I didn't have to organize anything for the night. Daddy Tripp took care of all of the details. He packed my clothes. He arranged the changing room. Everything. I was sure Elliot had a say in some of it. He was far more familiar with the place than I was and balanced an interesting role. He was little. There was no denying that, but he was also a caregiver of sorts for me at times. I thought of him as maybe a big brother more than a daddy, but the vibe was there.

All I had to do was be ready to go by six o'clock and I was…hours early. Six o'clock took forever and six weeks to get here, but finally, we were in the car and on our way.

I sat in the back seat with Elliot. Daddy Tripp looked like our chauffeur more than our daddy with us snuggled back there together. Normally, we took turns sitting next to him, but Elliot must have sensed that I needed company—or maybe he was just as excited as I was. But in either case, we sat in the back, holding hands tightly, bouncing up and down and giggling. So much giggling.

We were doing this, going to the place where this all began, this time as a committed triad.

Leaving when we did had us arriving before the bulk of the members, and we found a parking spot close to the entrance and checked in fairly quickly. Ms. Lily was at the front desk chatting when we got there and was excited to take us to our changing room, the one Daddy Tripp had booked for us.

I'd heard about all the different themes of the changing rooms, but nothing prepared me for when she opened the door to let us in. It was a full-on zoo theme. There was nothing subtle about it and I freaking loved it. The walls had murals filled with all different kinds of animals from around the world but not realistic ones. They were cartoonish and adorable. The changing table had decals of elephants and giraffes all over it. The containers holding supplies like individual use lube, condoms, packages of baby wipes, and diaper cream—all of those had different animals on them as well.

This place did not mess around.

I walked around, soaking it all in.

"I know you didn't feel comfortable bringing Koalakins here, but I thought this was close enough." Daddy hadn't picked it just because it was fun. He chose it specifically because he knew that it would help put me at ease. I wasn't surprised by this. He was always so thoughtful, but hearing it did have me up in my feels.

I threw my arms around him, and Elliot's came around me from behind for a huge Teddy-Elliot hug.

From there, Daddy helped us get dressed—first me then Elliot. We were wearing matching shirts, both brand new. They were tight and almost cropped-length with embroidered cookies on them.

I didn't think the cookies had a particular meaning as much as they matched—and they were cute. Or maybe he picked them because he wanted to get that cookie later. I needed to ask him, but not now. Now was about figuring out if playing at the club with Daddy Tripp like this was something we should do more often and if

Their Little House Boston

I wanted my own membership or if being a guest once in a while was enough.

Both Daddy and Elliot assured me that no decisions needed to be made tonight or even in the near future. That pressure was on me 100 percent by me. It was just how I was.

The first time we were here, Elliot and I were new friends and Daddy was a stranger. This time, we were already together, already comfortable with each other, and already loved each other. It was going to be so different and I was thrilled to experience how.

As we walked out with our knee highs covered in koalas, our short shorts, and our matching shirts, I knew we were in for the best night ever—or at least one of them. I seemed to have a lot of those with these two, and I didn't expect that to end any time soon.

Daddy took our hands, and we worked our way to the little room.

There were a few people in here, but not many. Ms. Lily was setting up a book for story time as we walked in. Miss Rebecca, who helped last time we were here, wasn't to be seen, but she'd probably show up. From what Elliot said, they tended to make sure that the same people were in the little room so people felt comfortable and safe.

Lorelei M. Hart

"What should we do first?" Daddy asked.

It was a no-brainer for me: blocks. Brick blocks like the ones in the little house playroom.

They were the first little toy I tried, the first one that helped me see how this kind of play could take the world away from me, and it felt only fitting for our first activity here. They had a ton more bricks than back in the playroom, and we spent at least an hour building a huge wall—both wide and tall. Daddy helped hold it in place as we went taller and wider until every brick was gone.

Then we let it fall and shatter everywhere, giggling before building it again.

Maybe it wasn't the most exciting activity in the room and definitely not for this club. Just the things I saw walking to the little room told me that. But it was absolutely perfect.

After our second wall was allowed to collapse and we picked the pieces up, we opted to join Ms. Lily's story time, and I was in the exact state of mind to experience it fully.

From there, the rest of the night was amazing, but that first activity…that was a memory I'd never forget. It was special in a way words couldn't express.

I felt loved. Cared for. But also like I'd finally found where I was supposed to be and who I was supposed to be with. Elliot and Tripp were my people. Most people were lucky to find love with one person, and somehow I'd managed to find it with two.

Chapter Twenty-One

Tripp

I'd invited them over to my house to watch a movie, but I think we all hoped it would be more than that. At least I did. The air between us was charged with sexual tension whenever we were together, and our foray into playing at Chained again was even better now that we knew one another well.

Spending the afternoon getting ready for our date, I was as nervous as a teenager with his first boyfriend. I knew about the popcorn salad at the little house from an invitation to join them one night, but I didn't think I could achieve Scottie's masterpiece—also, I found it a little intense for date night.

So, instead, I went another way, big food, but with a little twist.

A knock on the door startled me just as I finished my last bit of food artistry, and I covered the plate and set it in the refrigerator. *Okay. Whatever happens is good. If we end up in the bedroom, if we don't... It will still be a wonderful evening, so no pressure.*

I hadn't given myself a pep talk like that before a date since I was that teen boy back in the day. It was about as effective now as it had been then. But what did fix it, was opening the door to see Elliot and Boston on my front steps, holding hands, their expressions revealing anything but calm. My daddy side snapped into gear, putting their feelings first, and I offered them a broad smile. "Right on time! I picked out a few movies for us, and I hope you'll like one of them."

Boston nodded solemnly. "Whatever you like, I'm sure we will too."

"Oh no, not like that." I reached for their linked hands and used them to draw them inside. "We all have to agree. I picked one animation, one superhero, and one action movie. Come and see."

When we were seated on the sofa, I told them which I had in mind. "Of course, we can stream almost anything you like, I was just a little nervous and wanting to be all ready for your visit to my home."

A *whoof* from the backyard preceded the entrance of a very fluffy dog who was super excited to meet any and all workmen, guests, and anyone else who came through the door. Before I could stop her, she had her front paws on Elliot's thighs and a friendly dog-dog smile pointed at Boston.

"Oh, this is Juno!" Boston dropped to the floor cross-legged and held out his arms. Two seconds later, my dog and my boys were rolling around and having the best time ever. Juno and I had a great life together, but this dog wanted boys in her life as much as I did.

And my heart swelled even bigger with joy and an emotion we hadn't named yet but that I hoped I wasn't the only one feeling. Once the two were covered with fluff, I managed to convince them to sit on the sofa while I brought out our snacks. Juno stretched across both of their laps. She didn't belong on the couch, knew better, but from the furry state of the upholstery, she spent most of the time I was not with her, sleeping on it. There were a lot worse things a pup could do on her own, so I had given up on telling her not to.

Besides, the photo I took of the three of them would warm any winter's night.

"What are those?" Boston's jaw dropped. "That's fruit?"

Elliot clapped his hands. "I saw them on TikTok. Heart emoji fruit snacks! See?" He pointed to the plate. "The yellow part is pineapple, but it can be other things like mango or papaya, and the eyes are strawberries. These are...oh my gosh, you know we could do other emojis for house movie night. But what would we make the sunglasses out of?"

I had also brought out a mini grazing board with nuts, cheese, grapes, apples...various things that soon turned into a craft project as the two of them attempted to create all their favorite emojis. At first, they used TikTok on one of their phones, but then they decided it was cheating, or maybe they wanted to be more creative. Either way, I got to sit back and watch my men express their creativity on a whole different level.

Juno wandered off to eat her dinner in the kitchen eventually, and we ate all the artwork, cuddling on the sofa and making plans to wow everyone with their skill. They were even considering doing their own video to demonstrate. But then, it got quiet. The hilarity eased, and the atmosphere changed.

"Movie now?" I asked. "I think we need a break."

"Can we watch it in your bed, Tripp?" Elliot asked, resting his cheek on my shoulder.

"I don't have a screen in there," I said. "I'm sorry."

"Don't be." Boston stood up and reached out a hand to each of us. "We can make our own movie magic."

For a moment, I thought he really wanted to film us in bed, but then Elliot laughed. "No movies, but lots of magic, okay?"

I let out a breath of relief. Sex was great when it was in the moment, but the idea of watching myself in action made me shudder. Camera shy, much?

"Good. I want to concentrate on making you both feel good, not about what would look good on film...video...whatever."

My bed was a California King, plenty big enough for the three of us, and I might have bought new bedding for the occasion. Nobody commented on it, but I was far too focused on other things to care. Like the men who were shedding their clothes next to it. There was nothing little about these two at the moment, their toned bodies and not-little cocks making me feel a bit over my head. Could I be enough for both of them?

But the dynamic here was not a daddy and his two littles. It was three adult men who knew what they wanted in the bedroom, and once the kissing started, I no longer worried about who might satisfy whom. And when we were all giving one another blow jobs in a configuration I had no idea how we managed, I was ready to take back my doubts about filming our time in bed together. Because we were awesome.

Award-winning, possibly.

My heart pounded so hard, I was sure they could hear it, as we stopped before anyone came. "Condoms and lube in the nightstand," I said, hoping one of them was close enough to reach, and rewarded when the supplies landed on the mattress.

Boston lay on the bed, on his back, knees pulled up to his chest, and I helped prepare him, holding his cheeks apart while Elliot donned a condom and covered it in lube then inserted slippery fingers into his hole.

I was ready to come already, but when Elliot replaced his fingers with his cock, I got on my knees behind him and went to work on his hole. I'd never been with two men this way before, but it seemed so natural, so perfect, so complete, as we moved in tandem, Elliot in Boston, me in Elliot, and Boston stroking himself in perfect rhythm.

He went first, with a sharp cry that had my balls tightening. Elliot froze, gasping, and that was it for me, my cum spilling into the condom reservoir. Safety first, but bareback in a week or two was going to destroy my mind.

I braced myself on my hands, shivering in reaction before we all collapsed in a heap, kissing and panting and laughing a bit.

"Why did we wait so long?" Elliot asked, nibbling on Boston's throat.

"To be sure," the other man said, quivering.

"I'm sure," I said, stroking whatever I could reach, "that you were both worth waiting for."

Chapter Twenty-Two

Boston

Collapsing into a pile of sweaty limbs with Tripp and Elliot was not how I anticipated the evening ending. I thought we'd take it slow, like we had been. I'd never been so happy to be wrong. And now? Now, I was lucky enough to end up in the middle, with both of them snuggled up, one on each side of me. I was the center of the most perfect sandwich there was.

Simultaneously exhausted and wired.

Tripp kissed my forehead and announced that we needed to get cleaned up. Moving hadn't been in my immediate plans, but his suggestion was solid. Waking up a sticky gross mess in the morning wasn't my idea of a good time and even with the condoms, there was mess aplenty.

Slowly, I got out of bed with Elliot and Tripp, and we went into the bathroom, where he had a fairly decent-sized shower. We took turns washing each other's hair and each other's bodies, exploring our partners at a slower pace than we had in the bed.

Everything had happened so fast once we decided where the evening was headed. How could it not? We'd been wanting this for so long. Once we finally gave ourselves permission to go full-speed ahead, I loved every minute of it.

Once we were clean and rinsed, Tripp turned the water off and then, starting with Elliot, dried each of us off from head to toe. And then being the daddy that he was, offered us each a snack.

I wasn't hungry, though—not for food. The shower had woken me up again in multiple places, and I was ready to be pressed against my men once again. No, that wasn't what I wanted, longed for something else, and part of me was too scared to ask them for it. The other part of me couldn't wait to blurt it out.

"I think we lost him," Elliot teased.

I turned to Elliot, wondering what I'd missed while envisioning my guys making out while I watched.

"I don't know what you mean."

Both me and Tripp started laughing.

"You went away from us." Elliot tapped my nose. "What were you thinking about?"

This was my opening. "I-I'm not sure you wanna know." I was only half teasing. They would either love my idea or hate it. But one thing was for sure, they would never make me feel bad about it. Both of them were great about that.

"Now, you really need to tell us." Tripp intertwined his fingers with mine, anchoring me.

"I was thinking that you and Elliot look really hot when you kiss, and I kind of wanted to watch you do more than kissing."

"Oh really? And what was that more you'd want to see?" Elliot raised his eyebrow. He 10,000 percent knew and wanted to hear my words.

There was no judgment in his voice, just a sort of happy amusement mixed with some heat. I didn't know if he was going to like what I was about to say, but whatever the case may be, he appreciated that I was speaking freely based on the way his hand now rested on my chest.

I turned to Tripp. "I'd like to see you…inside him."

"Inside me?" Elliot ran his finger down my chest toward my already hardening cock. "Where should he be inside me? My mouth? My hole?"

Damn. I hadn't thought about that. "I don't care. Just…somewhere. Is that something that maybe we could do sometime, Daddy?"

The name filled the bathroom.

"Are you interested in seeing it now? Is that on the table?" Elliot's attention was no longer on me now; instead, he was watching Tripp.

"If that's what our boy wants, can we deny him?"

Me. I was our boy. I freaking loved it.

I dropped Tripp's hand and ran to the bedroom, where I dragged the small chair his suit jacket hung over toward the bed and took a seat. "I'm ready." So beyond ready. This wasn't the first time this scenario had run through my head, but it was the first time I allowed myself to acknowledge it, and that pushed me to share it.

Elliot shook his head in humor. "Looks like our boy wants a show. Let's give it to him."

I'd never been brave like this. I wasn't one to hide who I wanted or what my desires were, but this—this was so bold. So outside my norm. Then again, I'd gone from somebody who liked men and women to somebody who discovered that they were not only poly but also little—why not add voyeuristic to the mix?

Elliot climbed onto the bed. He crooked a finger for Tripp, and they both sat there on their knees, kissing, then hands wandering while small moans of pleasure escaped them. They managed to angle their bodies so I was able to see everything. They were putting on the show, and I was there for it.

They continued for a few minutes and then Tripp guided Elliot so he was flat on his back, his cock hard and bouncing with the motion of it. Tripp worked Elliot's cock with his mouth while he managed to coat his fingers with lube and work Elliot's entrance until he was squirming beneath Daddy, begging for more...and more Daddy gave him.

Tripp helped get Elliot situated so that he was bent over the back side of the bed and then slowly entered him. The angle was perfect for me to see him as he entered our partner. I could see every single movement from where I sat. He bottomed out and then slowly at first, he thrust in and out.

My hand went to my own cock, not even caring if they saw...maybe liking that they could. Letting me see what they were doing had me so turned on, how could I sit there and not take matters into my own hand.

I jerked in time as Tripp's tempo quickened. My cock was hard as nails, much quicker than it should have, given I had just come so recently, and my climax wasn't far behind. As cum coated my hand, Daddy reached beneath Elliot and grabbed his cock, helping him orgasm before he too exploded inside our mate.

It was the hottest thing I'd ever seen, ever participated in.

And I had a feeling our sex life was only going to get hotter from here.

Chapter Twenty-Three
Elliot

Tripp texted us in our group chat the night before. He wanted to take us to breakfast, since he didn't have any meetings and we both were working odd shifts and didn't go in until noon. It took work to get together while our schedules were different, and especially since two of us lived in another home from our daddy, but we made it work.

I wanted it to work more than anything.

"What are you wearing?" Boston came in without knocking. He'd seen me dressed and nude, so there was nothing to hide

"Just a T-shirt and shorts. It's so hot outside."

Boston smiled with one side of his mouth, looking very boyish. He and Tripp were truly the most beautiful men I'd ever known. "You look really good in that. Not that you don't in everything." We shared a quick kiss, and he hung out on my bed while I washed my face and got dressed. He took my hand in his, and we walked to his room where he got dressed, giving me a show while he did.

If Tripp wasn't waiting for us, we might not have gone out at all.

"Have you ever been to this place?" I asked, speaking of the restaurant Tripp insisted on. It had upscale diner offerings but only stayed open for breakfast and lunch. After that, it closed down.

"No. But I'm starving for French toast."

"I thought you were starving for me?" I laughed, edging my fingers up his thigh.

"Wait until we get home."

"Hmmm..."

Tripp stood up as we walked in the door. He sat between us in the curved booth as we decided what to have.

Once we'd ordered, he took our hands. "I'm so happy to see you two. I was hoping to discuss something with you next week, but I didn't sleep very well and thought I should talk to you about it today instead."

"Was it something bad?" Boston asked. "Is that why you couldn't sleep?"

"No. Well, I don't think so."

"Please tell us." I tugged on his hand. "I won't be able to eat until you do."

Tripp chuckled so low and deep, it tickled parts that had no business getting tickled in a packed restaurant. "Well, it wouldn't be good if my boys couldn't eat. I wanted to talk to you both about...I want you two to live with me. That was why I couldn't sleep last night. I wished you were with me, cuddled up in my arms. My bed feels so empty without you."

I already knew my answer, but I would let Boston reply first. I didn't want him to be pressured by my response. Tripp was everything I wanted in a daddy and a partner. I knew he loved us even though we hadn't said the words. Perhaps it was time to say those things.

"Are you sure?" Boston asked. "What happens if we get into an argument? If you're mad at me—at us."

Tripp turned to him. "If we have an argument or disagree with something, then we work it out, together. Gently. With love. I won't turn you out without a home just because we have a fight, Boston. What kind of daddy would I be if I did? What kind of a partner?"

"He would never," I supported. Boston knew it too. Tripp would never put us out no matter the reason.

A tear slid down Boston's face. "I had to say it, but I love you and I know you love us."

And just like that, he'd broached the subject.

"I love you both," Tripp said.

"And I love you both," I said. By the time our food arrived, we were all happily crying messes.

"Is it bold of me to assume you two want to move in?" Tripp asked.

"Not at all. When should I start packing?" Boston asked the question on the tip of my tongue. "We don't have a lot. We only have our clothes and personal items and a bit of furniture."

"How about this weekend? If I recall correctly, all of us are off."

"We are."

"Then, this weekend it is. Until then, how about you two start spending the night with me?"

We agreed and dug into our meals with gusto. The French toast was perfect. After we ate, it was time for all of us to get back to the real world but tonight, after Boston and I got off work, we would pack a bag and go sleep where we belonged, in the arms of the man who loved us.

Boston texted me several times during the day asking if I was excited and if it was okay when he got off his shift to start packing my stuff as well.

I had been sure he would be the hold up in this relationship, but I was excited to know he was happy as well. Enthusiastic, even.

Epilogue
Tripp

Having my littles under my roof changed everything. They brought such joy into the house, and reminded me of what had been missing in my life for so long. I'd had littles before, but they'd never lived with me, and it had only been one at a time. The frames they made the first night had pride of place on the mantel, one filled with a picture of the three of us and Juno, the other just our pup, drawn by Elliot because, as little Boston said, she was that important. Every time I looked at those frames, I remembered the night they made them and no amount of glitter shed that had to be swept up mattered.

Even as we grew together, I'd been unprepared for how much they would change my life. No more dinner meetings. They both had different schedules, but my day was eight hours and no more. That way, I could go home for dinner with whichever of them was home or, if I was lucky, they both were. And funny thing, when I told people I wasn't available in the evening, that I was due home to my family, they always managed a daytime appointment.

It paid to be firm.

We tried to make it to Chained one night a week, two or three of us to play or just to visit with like-minded folks, went to playdates once or twice a month, and dated each other often. But Saturday afternoons were for daddy/little play, and we did that in the new nursery. Completely magical times together.

"Daddy, we don't have bubbles," called Boston. "My duckies won't get in the tub."

"I'm sure we have some." Mostly because I kept an extra bottle hidden away. Elliot and Boston had a tendency to pour way too much bubble bath into the water the second my back was turned.

"I found it, Boston," Elliot called.

I'd already started the water and left for a moment to answer the phone, but when I reentered the bathroom, it was to find a bathtub crowned with mountains of bubbles and no littles in sight. Schooling my voice, I said, "Oh no. Boston and Elliot are missing, and I came in here to wash their hair."

Giggles emerged from the depths of the tub. There was at least a half a bottle in there to create the effect, but it was worth it for their delight.

"Hmm, Daddy hears something, but I don't see any little boys. I'd better look for them." I left the room, calling their names, and listening to their laughter behind me. Returning to the bathroom, I sat down on the closed toilet seat and sighed. "Oh well. I guess I'll have to put posters up for missing little boys. I hope they'll be okay. They're going to miss their favorite dinner."

They both surged upward, sending bubbles flying. Much easier to clean up on the tile than finger paints, clay or glitter, for sure. And their smiles were so broad, their eyes twinkling, it was the most fun even though it was a game they played often.

"We're here, Daddy!" Boston crowed.

"We fooled you!" Elliot added.

"I see that!" Dropping to my knees, I soaped up a washcloth. "I'd better wash you both before you disappear again and miss your dinner entirely."

Rubbing the soapy cloth over their skin, I told them how glad I was to find them safe and sound. Then I passed out some new duckies and boats to add to their flotilla and distract them while I washed each boy's hair. Then I settled back to watch them play until the water cooled. Once again, I blessed whoever put this tub in because we sure got a lot of use out of it.

Their Little House Boston

Then I helped them out one by one, dried them carefully, and dressed them in footie jams. "Naptime, my bestest boys," I said, guiding them into the nursery.

"Not sleepy, Daddy," Boston said, rubbing his eyes.

"Then I guess you don't want a bottle." I shrugged, hiding my smile while they scrambled to their double crib and held their arms up for me to help them in. Boston and Elliot cuddled together, and I handed them the bottles I'd prepared while they were looking for bubble bath. "You're such good boys."

Elliot pulled his bottle from his mouth. "Don't go 'way, Daddy."

"Never." I kissed them each on the forehead and settled in the glider right next to the crib. "Story?"

Their library was growing all the time as they spotted books with beautiful illustrations and intriguing concepts. As my boys drifted off into dreamland, I set the book on my lap and leaned my head back to rest my eyes for a few minutes. Our Saturday afternoons were my favorite time of the week, but these two boys could sure make a daddy tired by the time they were over.

Not that I'd ever complain. In an hour or so, they'd be awake and wanting either nuggies or steak and shrimp, depending on whether they were still in little space. I was prepared to enjoy either.

After my nap.

An Excerpt from *Their Little House Tristan*

What happens in Little House, stays in Little House.

In theory, I'm graduating this spring, but *in theory* doesn't pay tuition, and when my scholarship is canceled at the last minute, I have no choice but to put my education on hold. I pack my bags and move back home, where my parents are not what a person could call understanding about my sexuality. I couldn't imagine what they'd think if they found out I was little.

I luck out, getting a great job at Chained, one that includes a membership, but when they find out who's signing my paycheck, my parents give me an ultimatum: quit or move. Thankfully, one of the people at work lets me know about a house share where all the residents are little.

I'm in a place where I can truly be myself for the first time. Sure, things get a tad awkward when one of the other littles kisses me at Chained one night, but the way the hot daddy in the corner is watching us...I think I might need more of his sweet kisses. A whole lot more.

Their Little House Tristan is the second book in the Five Little Roommates series by USA Today bestselling author Della Cain and her bestie Kaytea Kat. Tristan is an M/M/M daddy little romance featuring not one but two littles, the daddy who loves them both, a house full of littles with no daddy in sight, bottles, stuffies, onesies, true love, an adorable dog, the day at Chained that changes everything, chickie nuggies, mischief, and all the fun and sweetness you have come to expect from Della and Kaytea. If you love your daddies sweet, your littles fun, and your HEAs wrapped like a hug, grab Tristan today.

Chapter One

Tristan

"Are you packing?" My roommate, Pierre, put his arms over my suitcase to prevent me from adding more into it.

"I am—" It was the last thing I wanted to be doing, but it was outside my control.

I reached behind me, grabbed the letter that had just been delivered to me, and handed it to him. As he read it, I continued packing. There was nothing he'd find in the letter that would change the result, and I was on a time crunch—one not of my own making.

"This is bullshit." He tossed it on the bed. "They can't just cancel your scholarship after the semester began. They can't do that!"

"Except they did." I didn't think it was possible either, but according to everyone I'd been able to contact in the office, it was not only possible, but it impacted four of us. "I guess the foundation who sponsored it went under or something."

I hadn't really been able to focus after I was told it was real, and there was no way to fix the situation that didn't include me writing a big fat check.

"They said I have till tomorrow to pay or be kicked from classes. And there's no way I'm going to be able to afford it. Between the dorm and the tuition, we're looking at over $20,000."

His jaw dropped. "But, Tristan, you're graduating in a few months."

"No. No, I'm not." And that was the harsh reality of it—all this hard work, all this time, and now it ended just like that. All because of my stupid scholarship.

I'd already talked to the office and e-filed all the paperwork needed to take a leave of absence. It wasn't ideal, but they suggested it with the idea that some better financial aid could come through next year, or I somehow might manage to save enough to come back. But for now, I was done with the collegiate life.

And the reality was, I wasn't sure which was worse: losing three and a half years' worth of hard work, or being homeless with the only place left to go— my parents' home. Sadly, I was pretty confident it was the latter.

My parents were not what I would call understanding of who I was, and that was putting it lightly. They were in denial. Full-on denial.

In their mind, I wasn't attracted to boys. That was a phase I was going to outgrow. I was confused, rebelling, or misunderstanding my own attractions—the excuse depended on the day.

In their mind, after I graduated, I would marry a nice girl from the church—their church, obviously—and we'd have a gaggle of children, go to services twice a week with smiles on, and sit beside them in the pew. They had had my life planned out for me before I was even born. The only part of it that changed over the years was going to college because, for me, that had been nonnegotiable.

It was such a warped little picture of who we should be, formed by their own messed-up views on what made a "man" and not who their son was. And yet, no matter how much I tried to tell them otherwise, that's how they were determined my life would go.

I'd sworn when I went to college, I'd never go back. But I had no choice, at least not for now. It was go home or be homeless and as much as they bugged me, they weren't evil. They just didn't understand who

I was and had no desire to change that because it messed with their world view.

I could only imagine what they would think if they found out that my favorite thing in the world was to dress up in a onesie and diaper and suck on a paci while some sexy older daddy made me chickie nuggies or cuddled me as cartoons played in the background. I'd be shocked if they even knew littles existed. They lived in their own small world, one I'd come to realize I'd never be a part of.

"You don't have to go today, do you?"

"I do." And had already arranged my ride.

He walked around the bed and hugged me tight. "I wish we had gotten an apartment this year. Then you could stay."

I'd wished that too, but the money didn't work—not when the scholarship included this room. We had crunched numbers, and the hours we would have to work to make it happen weren't doable, not with our course loads and planned internships.

"It'll be fine," I lied. "I'll get a job, save the money, and finish next year."

"And your parents?"

"My parents will just...I have to be—I just need a place to stay while I get a job." Things with my parents were going to be tricky, but it wasn't like I could change that.

"And when they try to set you up with girls, you…"

"Well, obviously, I'll be too busy with my job." Would that work? I doubted it, at least not completely. But all I had to do was buy some time.

Pierre understood my situation all too well. He'd grown up in a household similar to mine, which was probably why, as freshmen, we clung to each other. His parents hadn't agreed with his choice of career. They wanted him to go into the medical field, specifically to become a doctor, and then ideally come back to *their* small town, find a nice girl in their church, get married, and live out their ideal dream.

Instead, Pierre went to school for English, or, as, his father said, "to waste your time and money." But, unlike me, my roommate's scholarship was still intact, and he was already accepted into a very prestigious graduate program for the next year. I was happy for him, but I'd be lying if I said I didn't wish I had a similar program waiting for me, or at least had the funds to finish this year.

We chatted as I packed up the rest of my things and went outside to meet my parents. They pulled up less than a half hour later with *I told you so* looks on their faces. They were not big believers in education, thinking that I could just get a job and already be living my "grown-up life." The scholarship was the only thing that had made me being here possible. My parents refused to so much as pay for SAT fees, much less anything once I was accepted to college.

"Thanks for coming to get me." I slapped on my happy face, the one I was going to have to hold on to for the next few months while I saved up.

"It's about time you came home." My mom hugged me.

My dad slapped me on the shoulder. "And just in time! We invited Sally Beth and her parents over for Sunday dinner."

"Sally Beth?" I had no idea who they were talking about.

"Yes, Sally Beth. The Stansted daughter."

It took me a few seconds to piece together who they were talking about and, when I did, my stomach roiled. How could they want that for me? "Isn't she a child?"

"You've been gone a long time. She turns eighteen next month." My mom said it as if that made it less gross.

"Oh." Because I couldn't afford to tell them how I really felt. At least, not yet. I'd just need to master the art of pivoting away from their matchmaking. It was gonna be a long couple months if they were already starting with this.

"If I don't have a job by then, I'll be happy to join you." Happy being a bald-faced lie.

"If you're living in our house, Son, you will not be working on Sundays." My father didn't pretend I had any say in it. "Sunday dinners are mandatory."

"Understood." I only had to do this for a few months. That was it. Nothing more. I could do anything for a few months, right?

Chapter Two

Bellamy

There are two rooms open.

I finished up my work for the law firm but knew that no matter how much I got done, there would always be more. My daytime job was never-ending and filled to the brim with anxiety, pressure, and overwhelming business. I didn't get as much little time as I wanted.

I gave my paralegal team a to-do list at nearly eight at night, right as I was about to go home. The team consisted of women and men fresh out of law school and some of them still working on their degrees. If I asked it of them, they would work all night, but I knew better. I wasn't like the other lawyers in the firm. That would only make them work slower the next day, and they would grow to resent me.

Their work would suffer. They were my legs on the ground. I needed them just as much as the firm needed me. If they were unhappy, I was unhappy and vice versa.

"Go on home," I said, placing a stack of papers and folders on their shared table. "Get some rest. Tomorrow is a big day and next week, we go to trial."

The group stood up, all smiling, and some of them high-fived each other. I walked with them to the elevator. They were making plans for dinner and drinks, but I didn't expect an invitation, of course. Dinner and drinks were no fun if you invited the boss, which was weird because I was their age. I finished high school at sixteen and law school at twenty-four. I was immediately picked up by a local firm, so the team in the elevator with me, well, most of them were my age or older.

It could've been awkward, but we respected one another. Made it work.

But still, going out with the boss wasn't cool no matter what age I was.

"What are your plans for tonight, Bellamy?" I'd nipped the sir nonsense in the bud the day each one started.

"You all know me." They absolutely didn't. "I'm going home to relax and enjoy my rest."

They laughed but didn't press for any further information. I didn't lie exactly. I was going to go home and enjoy my rent. How I chose to spend my free time was none of their business. My private life was just that.

After picking up a meal from a new restaurant that offered the best kids' meals in town, I drove home but wasn't as happy as I once was, going to what we all called the Little House. Of course, it was a safe space for us, but things had changed of late.

The house seemed lonelier since Colter and Dallas moved out to be with their forever daddy. I was happy for them, but it left the house a bit quiet. Less activity. Movie nights weren't as fun. There were more chores with fewer renters.

I wished some new littles would move in so I could have some new friends. Even the toys in the playroom were getting boring.

Ugh, I really needed to stop complaining so much.

At home, I sat down at the table to eat. Still wound tightly from work, I would have to unwind before I could even enjoy myself.

"Up for a movie later?" Monroe, the owner of the house we all lived in, sat across from me.

I sighed. "I don't know. What did you want to watch?"

"The anime cartoon we've been following. There's a new episode."

"That's not a movie," I laughed around a bite of creamy macaroni and cheese. The highlight of the meal was tiny corn dogs, but I'd put down a dozen of those immediately. They had given me a chocolate lava cake with the meal, and it was calling my name.

"Oh, that's true. But we could watch one after the episode."

I nodded.

His brow furrowed. "Bell, what's wrong?" My roommates were the only ones who could call me Bell and get away with it.

"I don't want to complain."

"Just tell me how you feel. Is this about Colter and Dallas moving out?"

I polished off my macaroni and cheese and offered Monroe some of my cake. He grabbed a spoon and a couple of juice boxes for us and joined me. "It's just quieter around here. Not as fun."

He nodded. "I get that. I've placed ads all over the place, but we haven't gotten many bites. I hope we can find someone soon. Are the chores too much for you? I can pick some of yours up if that's the problem. You work so many crazy hours. You must be exhausted."

"It's not that. I don't know. Sometimes I feel like I don't really fit in here."

Monroe stopped chewing. I thought he might scold me, but he cocked his head to the side. "You don't? I think you are a great fit. The others really seem to like you."

I didn't realize anyone liked me. I thought they were just being nice.

"Still, I hope we get some more roommates soon."

"Is the rent a problem? You know that I would never raise the rent just because someone moved out. Your rent and everything about your rental agreement stays the same."

"I know. I'm just tired. I think I'll go change into my jammies and take you up on that movie offer. When I come back down, I'll gather the snacks."

"Sounds good. I'm really glad you're here. Just so you know."

"Thanks."

I ran upstairs and took a quick shower. There was something about the law office and their air-conditioning system that left a film of scent on me. I smelled like office and didn't like it one bit.

Once I got out, I hung up my suit and prepared another for the next day just in case I fell asleep during the movie and didn't want to do anything else.

Downstairs, I popped popcorn and drizzled it with caramel then sprinkled salt over that. It was one of Monroe's favorites, and he had been kind to me, not only today but ever since I moved in. Along with that, I took out a package of mini donuts and a couple of tiny waters. We had enough sugar as it was.

The other thing about having fewer roommates was that more people distracted me from my loneliness. Sure, I was happy for my friends and their new daddy, but I wanted to find my own to take care of me and be my partner in life.

Some days, it seemed like I might never find that person.

What a sad thought.

"Here we are," I announced to Monroe but, as I came around the corner, I saw everyone had joined in for the fun. More people meant I felt even more out of place. It wasn't them. They had tried to include me in every facet of living in this place.

I simply never felt good enough.

"Thank you, Bellamy," they all replied in unison.

"You're welcome," I said sheepishly and sat down in a chair while the rest of them sat together on a couch or on the floor. Everyone had their jammies on and were comfortable. This was where we relaxed and let the knots and stress of the day go away.

As soon as the cute, upbeat music of the new episode came on, my spirits immediately lifted. The issues remained, but for now, I was comfortable and happy.

And free to be me.

About the Authors

By day, Della Cain writes sugary sweet with a dash of heat caregiver romances about littles and their daddies, pups and their masters, and everything in between.

By night, their life is a bit more tame. They enjoy baking, cute pens, stuffies, kawaii, oh, and of course puppies and kitties! Basically, anything that makes their heart happy while bringing a smile to their face. Della hopes they give their readers that same warm-hearted feeling with each of their books...along with a naughty little tickle.

***

Kaytea Kat writes stories about adorable littles and their strong, protective daddies/caregivers that let them explore both sides of their relationship in whatever way makes them happiest. Even if it means there's lots of glitter to be cleaned up after a play session...or maybe especially those times.

Their Little House Boston

She loves gardening and baking and watching old movies where love conquers all. Because she believes that it just might.

Made in United States
Cleveland, OH
16 March 2026